Fireline has everything a good non-stop action book should have... A delightful story with plenty of action, heart-pounding romance, and a mystery that keeps on ticking.

KELLY, GOODREADS

Fast paced from beginning to end, this is a book you'll not want to put down.

LILY, GOODREADS

This book was a whirlwind and I loved it. Fire, secrets, and fast paced on the action, we get a HEA for two characters that have been dancing around each other this series. I loved delving into their pasts and putting a lot of pieces to our series long mystery into place. I couldn't put this book down. I read it cover to cover in a single sitting. I'm eagerly awaiting the final installment!

MICHAELA, GOODREADS

Fireline had it all! Fire, action, spies and nail-biting moments. Be sure to lock yourself away to finish this book.

SARITA, GOODREADS

FIRELINE

CHASING FIRE MONTANA | BOOK 5

A SERIES CREATED BY SUSAN MAY WARREN AND LISA PHILLIPS

KATE ANGELO

Fireline
Chasing Fire: Montana, Book 5

Print ISBN: 978-1-963372-17-5
EBOOK ISBN: 978-1-963372-16-8

For more information about Kate Angelo please access the author's website at kateangelo.com

Published in the United States of America.
Cover Design: Lynnette Bonner

For God, Who fills me daily with unimaginable peace and joy.

For Jerry, my prayer warrior, trusted advisor,
biggest supporter, and best friend.

And for Daniel and Teresa, loving parents to this orphan.

"Come to me, all you who are weary and burdened, and I will give you rest. Take my yoke upon you and learn from me, for I am gentle and humble in heart, and you will find rest for your souls."
Matthew 11:28-29 (NIV)

But Lord, 'tis for Thee, for Thy coming we
wait,
The sky, not the grave, is our goal;
Oh, trump of the angel! Oh, voice of the
Lord!
Blessed hope, blessed rest of my soul.

ONE

HIS ENEMIES HAD FOUND HIM.

All this time and they'd come so far. They'd nearly finished it.

Now it would all be for nothing.

The plane dropped about a hundred feet somewhere over the Kootenai National Forest. Okay, maybe it was fifty. Twenty. Booth Wilder didn't know. Turbulence mixed with dread and exhilaration of what he was about to do left him nauseated.

The six-man crew of smokejumpers was packed in tight. Shoulder to shoulder. All crowded around the windows according to their jump order.

Booth sat with Nova Burns, a thrill-seeking legacy smokejumper with a propensity toward bossiness. Behind them were Finn and Vince, the two sawyers who'd be out front clearing the brush for the crew. Last in line was Logan, the team lead, and JoJo, another seasoned smokejumper.

He glanced at the stoic faces. These jumpers, they had families, homes, lives outside the smoke. Booth wasn't even sure who he was anymore. Just a

WITSEC nobody. No past, no future, just this endless free fall until Homeland gave him back his life.

"You good?" Nova shouted into the side of his helmet.

"Better if Aria didn't plow through every air pocket like she was flyin' an F-22," he yelled over the roar of the engines. "I miss Tirzah!"

"Whatever. Aria is every bit a daredevil pilot. We were lucky to get her from Alaska!" She shouted into her headphone mic, "Hey, Aria! Ever think of becoming a fighter pilot?"

"Why you think I carry a .357 Magnum?" Her voice crackled over the intercom. "I just stick my arm out the window and pew pew pew."

Laughter filled the fuselage but cut off when the plane hit another patch of turbulence. They slammed down on the cargo. The mirth turned to grumbling.

Vince rubbed his elbow. "For real. If Aria doesn't take it easy, I'll have to jump outta this plane."

"Please tell me someone packed Huggies in the cargo box for Vince." Their spotter for the day, Eric Dale, laughed over the intercom.

Booth peered out the window. The charred remains of the mountain landscape rushed past at a hundred miles an hour. Thousands of lush green acres lay blackened, ravaged by the wildfire. To the west, black veins of ash pulsed through a crimson expanse.

Somewhere out there in the endless wilderness was the real Crazy Henry from the stories Booth told by the fire.

And Crispin.

Three years since the nuke had gone missing.

Three years since his life had fallen apart.

They'd said his former partner was dead. So why was Crispin here, in Ember of all places?

Was his appearance connected to Earl's death? Was this where the nuke trail led? If Crispin was playing some deep game, Booth needed to see the board. Maybe finding him would lead him to the nuke, and maybe it would lead him back to himself.

He had to find Crispin. That was the goal. But how? This town was a haystack, and he was searching for the needle blindfolded.

The plane bounced and fell again. Queasiness sloshed around his stomach. His breathing was tight, restricted by the straps on his jump harness. He'd never been so eager to jump from a plane before.

"Still good?" Nova nudged his knee.

"Fine. Just…thinking."

The plane winged down into a hard turn. They turned their attention back to the windows as the plane circled the fire, giving them a closer look. Two hundred acres of fierce flames shot out from the trees, sending billows of dense black smoke spiraling into the sky. Booth's chest constricted. The fire raged in every direction.

Eric left his seat from the cockpit and picked his way through the tangle of jumpers. At the door, he attached the restraining line to his harness so that if he fell out, they could pull him back in. Booth had seen it happen once, so he'd never forget the restraining line.

"Guard your reserves!" Eric yelled.

Booth and every other jumper covered their reserve chute with a forearm to protect it from accidental deployment when the door opened. Booth had seen that happen too.

Eric grabbed the handles and twisted. The door hinged back toward the tail of the plane. Cold air and the scent of woodsmoke rushed in.

Nova stood at the jump doors, face hidden behind the wire-mesh guard on her helmet. "Fire's about twenty-five miles northeast of Snowhaven. Wind conditions aren't much better than yesterday, and the head is pushing southwest toward an area with a few homesteads."

"They've called for evacuations," Logan said. "But we know not everyone takes it seriously."

"Yeah, there's always one who thinks they can ride it out," Finn said.

"Buddy check," Nova said, pulling on her fire gloves. "Booth's with me first stick. Logan and Vince, second stick. JoJo and Finn, third."

Booth went to the door and performed his four-point check.

Nova stuck her head out of the plane beside Eric. Booth watched over Nova's shoulder as Eric dropped the first set of drift streamers. They watched them fall. The long pieces of weighted crepe paper fell toward the ground, catching on currents.

Booth did some quick mental calculations and determined wind drift and descent time. "Looks good?"

Eric nodded his agreement. "Aria, take us to three thousand!"

Aria's voice crackled over the intercom. "We're at three thousand."

"All right. Looks like about a hundred fifty yards of drift. The wind is strongest down low. Stay wide of the fire." Eric's head swung out the opening, then he turned back. "Get in the door!"

Booth backed up to give Nova room. She sat on the floor and braced herself. Her feet dangled out into the slipstream, ready to jump into the vast canvas of the sky. He dropped into position and moved in tight behind her. The hum of the plane vibrated under his legs. Nova leaned back. Pressed herself into his chest.

The familiar tingle of raw energy electrified his muscles. Nerves firing. Blood pumping. Countless jumps and he couldn't shake the mix of fear and exhilaration seconds before the free fall. He took a deep breath. The crisp air filled his lungs. This was it. The moment before the plunge.

Eric's slap came down on Nova's shoulder, and she propelled herself forward out into the wind.

Booth rocked forward as hard as he could to miss the edge of the door but bumped it on the way out. He tumbled under the tail of the plane in a slow spin and turned his belly to the ground.

The rush of wind, the weightlessness, and the deafening roar of the air enveloped him. In that moment, all fear and doubt were left behind. His past mistakes were replaced by the freedom of flight. He had nothing but the sky and the guilt of surviving when others hadn't.

He counted in his head and kept his eyes on the horizon. "Jump thousand...look thousand...reach thousand...wait thousand..."

Once stable, he pulled the rip cord. "Pull thousand!"

A hard jerk pulled at his chest straps. The parachute riffled open high above the burning landscape. For a moment there was nothing but Booth, the wind in his ears, and the land below. Nothing but him and the God who had spoken all this into being. The wildfire ravaged the divine canvas, but underneath it all, there was a promise of renewal and rebirth.

This was the part he loved. He'd come to Ember looking for a place to lay low, but jumping had gotten into his blood. But did he love it enough if the time came for him to choose between this life and the dead one?

He grabbed the steering toggles and turned to face the hundreds of miles of wilderness. Smoke rose high overhead, gathering in storm clouds. Violent flames whipped back and forth between the trees.

Nova was right. This thing had the potential to go big. The other crews needed all the help they could get. They needed him.

Booth descended through open sky. The only audible sounds were the distant hum of the jump ship and the gentle flutter of his parachute as he glided twenty-five hundred feet above the earth.

"Oooooh-weeeee!" Nova yelled.

Booth grinned and let out his own whooping shout.

Between his feet, wind whipped Nova's chute to the west. She swept over a dense stand of towering Douglas firs. He caught the same wind gust and steered hard, but the wind pulled him toward the same trees.

Facing into the wind, he tried to locate the jump spot through the thick smoke.

The chute rocked back and forth. Booth's gut tightened.

He pulled down on the left toggle and moved closer to the wind line. The strong smell of smoke filled the air and stung his nostrils.

Two hundred feet to go and he could barely see the ground through the dense ash cloud. "I can't see the spot!"

"It's gonna be a hanger!" Nova hollered something else he couldn't hear.

Another headwind blew him backward and into the woods. This was turning out to be more dangerous than catching bad guys. Forget making the spot. He just needed to land somewhere without hanging up.

At a hundred feet, things got worse. The wind died and he moved forward, but it was too late to clear the trees. He entered the opening at treetop level just in time to see Nova crash into a thick stand of birch and disappear.

Barely missing some of the taller trees, he reefed down on his left toggle and flew between two towering trunks. His canopy brushed trees, tearing and snagging on smaller branches as he passed. Instead of slowing down, he began to speed up in a free fall.

The ground was steep, and he teetered on the edge of slamming into it. All this time doing the right thing, biding his time, holding himself apart from the world, for it to end like this.

And there was nothing he could do about it.

Nova's parachute billowed above her, snagging branches on the way down. The world became a blur of green and brown, branches whipping past. Her boot clipped a tree branch. The choked scream died in her throat.

This was it. Her legacy. Another smiling portrait on the memorial wall back at jump base.

The thick fabric caught and sent a jolt running through her body as she jerked to a stop. She swung back and forth, suspended six feet above the unforgiving earth.

Six feet. Six feet from being another memory for someone. Six feet from another empty space at the dinner table.

Nova closed her eyes and blew out a tight breath. That was ridiculous. "You're a smokejumper, Nova. This is what you do. You survive."

But what if *they* didn't?

Nerves had her hands shaking as she put the drogue release in her pocket. "Booth, am I safe to let down?" She looked around but didn't see him.

"Booth?"

Overhead, tree limbs rustled. Booth plummeted down between two big birch trees, grunting and growling all the way down. Branches ripped at his jump gear and tore his chute.

"Booth!"

Calling his name was dumb. All she could do was hang there and watch him fall end over end through the trees and pray his gear did its job.

His arms and legs snagged branches, broke loose, and he got hung up again. The chute caught a limb and jerked him over. He landed head down between two branches, suspended inches off the ground.

He swung there for a second, then laughed. "At least I didn't hit the—"

A branch cracked. The chute pulled loose. Booth came crashing down into the underbrush and hit the ground. A second later he rolled to his back and groaned.

Nova winced. "Ouch. Are you okay?"

Booth's thumb shot up.

"Hang on, I'm coming down." Nova found her letdown tape in a leg pocket and threaded it between the V formed by her riser. "Inside, outside. Outside, inside."

The chant helped her remember to route the tape over the top of the main letdown line and secure herself to the riser. She tied off using three half hitches and ran the rest of the tape. She did the five-point check and released the risers.

She eased down, letting the tape slide through her gloved hands in a smooth descent. Her boots hit the forest floor, and she pulled her helmet off.

Nova ran to Booth and leaned over him. "Seriously, are you hurt? That looked painful."

"Wow. I didn't know you cared." Booth got to his feet and pulled his helmet off to reveal a toothy smile. He tossed his disheveled hair. "Good jump, huh?"

"Good jump? We could've broken our necks."

"Hey, anything I walk away from is a good jump in my book." The shadow of something unspoken passed over his eyes. "I'm just glad we're both safe."

"Yeah, me too."

Nova called the plane and let them know their status. "Visibility is shot with all this smoke. And the wind gusts are a bit worse than we thought. Remind the crew of letdown procedures, because they'll probably get treed up."

"Ten-four," Eric said. "The rest of the crew is coming down in a new jump spot with better visibility." He gave her the coordinates and she confirmed.

Nova checked the navigation. Two paths looked promising.

She grabbed her helmet and secured it to her pack. "Ridge. It's quicker."

"Hold on, Wildfire Girl." Booth dusted himself off. "That's a steep, rocky climb and closer to the fire. We could get cut off. Let's take the forest."

"It's too dense. We'll spend hours cutting through the underbrush."

"It's safer than us being trapped like sitting ducks," Booth said, packing his chute with a bit more force than needed.

Why was he always so stubborn? "Look, the fire won't wait. Your route will take twice as long, and that's precious time we don't have. We're taking the ridge. Grab your gear and let's go."

"Fine." Booth nodded, a flicker of something unreadable in his eyes. He hoisted his pack and set off.

As she followed Booth on the rocky trail, Nova couldn't shake the feeling that her voice, her decision, was lost in the smoke. It'd be nice if maybe, just once, Booth would listen to her instead of looking at her like she was a loose cannon waiting to explode.

It wasn't like this was her first rodeo. Following in her uncle Jock's footsteps, she'd joined the hotshot crew in high school and dug an uphill line for three years, followed by three more on the helitack crew before she'd made smokejumper. Booth had only… wait, she wasn't even sure of his history.

That man was nothing but a mystery sometimes.

They hiked the ridgeline for about six miles,

keeping a hard eye on the fire. The entire time, Nova ran fire entrapment training videos through her mind. If the fire started to overrun them, she had two or three escape routes planned.

They found the clearing about an hour later. Nova dropped her spent chute and her gear. She took an assessing glance at her team. All but one cargo drop had been unloaded, but by the looks of it, Vince, JoJo, and Finn would have it done in no time.

Logan carried a box of water on his shoulder, looking like the perfect hero some people seemed to think he was. He set the box down and grinned. "Glad you could join us."

"Gnarly landing, and a bit of a hike here, but we're in one piece." Nova flicked a glance at Booth, but he didn't chime in. "How 'bout you guys?"

"Came down with far less flair." Logan waved a hand at the boxes. "We've got the gear inventoried, and we're about to pack what we need for this trip."

"We got a firsthand look at the fire coming down," Nova said. "We've got a steep slope, so we can start in with a direct saw line at the tail and work up. Redirect the fire north." She clapped her hands. "Let's pack up and head out, ASAP."

In under an hour, they had all their gear to the tail of the fire. It was midafternoon, and if Nova was sweating, the rest of them were probably drenched. "Grab some water before we put together a strategy."

Nova drank from her canteen and studied the fire that burned some fifty feet away, beyond a meadow where the smokejumpers had already cut a wide line. From here she was safe, but the heat was intense, even with the distance.

"Okay, team, looks like the fire is a little over two

acres. Totally doable if the wind doesn't push us." She slid the map from her pocket and laid it on the ground. "Right in this area, there are two homesteads in the path of the fire. First priority is to save any locals who didn't evac."

"There's another house way out here." Logan tapped the map northeast. "The fire's pretty far and pushing south, so shouldn't be a problem."

Nova nodded. "Good. Once we get the line cut here, Logan, take JoJo and go up the right flank. Booth, Vince, and Finn, you guys hit the left. I'll scout the head of the fire and check the homesteads."

"I think it's better if I go with you," Booth said. "It's safer if we stay in pairs, and I can help once we get to the head."

Had Booth ever taken a single order without second-guessing her? "I can handle myself—"

"He's got a point," Logan said. "It's nothin' but a big spot fire. We can handle it, can't we?"

JoJo, Vince, and Finn voiced their agreement in unison.

She clenched her teeth and bit back the snarky comment threatening to fly out. Logan took Booth's side and encouraged the rest of the team to do the same. He might be aiming to beat her out as new crew chief, but she was team lead for this fire.

She looked at Booth. "I guess if the team can manage without you, then you're with me."

Logan clapped his gloved hands together. "Okay, let's secure this tail!"

Flames leaped up from the trees lining the southern perimeter. Billowing columns of dense black smoke rolled through the air, dimming the sun to a dull red. Crackles and hisses emanated from the dead trees and fallen logs.

Nova keyed the radio to contact Commander Miles Dafoe to check on the air attack. They could use a water drop.

Vince sized up a birch tree for about twenty seconds. He cranked up his chainsaw and dogged in. The man was a magician with a saw. And with a father as a captain in Cal Fire, fire had probably been his whole life like it had been for Nova.

Finn, the youngest on the team, went to work cutting out the brush and downed logs. The rest of the crew started in with their Pulaskis, scraping away the forest litter down to mineral soil to make a barrier that would be hard for the fire to cross.

An hour later, Nova and Booth weren't far from the first homestead when she heard a plane rumbling in the sky.

Her radio crackled. "Burns, we're coming up on your area. Clear for drop?"

She checked with Logan, and he confirmed they were all outside the drop zone. "Ten-four, tanker. We're clear for drop."

"Copy."

The plane rumbled in low. Overhead, there was a brilliant flash, and the air filled with rain. The water came down over the forest behind them.

"Let's move," Nova said to Booth. "The wind is pushing the fire fast. I'd like to get to those homesteads before it does." Their best hope was to get to the houses and make sure the owners had evacuated.

She trailed behind Booth, stepping over rocks and branches and using her Pulaski as a walking stick.

They kept roughly a hundred yards from the fire. Enough so they could keep an eye on it, but still close enough to feel the heat on the side of her face.

They walked maybe a mile through dense forest. The fire had slowed with the water drop. The air was not quite as smoky when they arrived at the narrow dirt driveway.

"There it is." She jogged past Booth to a small cabin with a lean-to porch and knocked on the door. "Anyone home?"

Booth cupped his hands and pressed his face to the window. "It's empty."

"You sure?"

"Yeah. Looks like a one-room hunting cabin." He pointed to an upright wooden rectangle over to the right of the cabin with a moon carved into the door. "Outhouse."

"Huh. Must be a hotshot, or someone who knows about wildland firefighting." Nova nodded to the twelve-inch-wide trench encircling the property.

"That's some fire line," Booth said. "How far to the next?"

"Half mile. Hydrate and let's go."

Booth struck out ahead, his long legs making the hustle easier for him. "You really think anyone's there?"

"You'd be surprised." She tried not to huff and puff with the heat and the exertion. "People are crazy about protecting their property."

He stepped over a fallen tree blocking the path. "That sounds like personal experience talking."

Nova's heart stuttered a beat. It was personal experience talking, wasn't it?

Her parents had refused to abandon their

livelihood to a wildfire and died trying to save it. Even though it'd meant leaving her behind. They'd chosen the homestead over her. "Everyone finds their worth in something. Homes, jobs, kids, relationships. Sometimes it's to their own detriment."

He shot a glance over his shoulder.

She squinted. "What's that look for?"

"Nothing. I mean, you're right." He skirted a boulder and used a tree limb to steady himself. "No one would stay up in these mountains without a really good reason."

"People go into the wilderness to find solitude and serenity." As if anyone ever could. Not completely.

"I heard you grew up on a homestead in the mountains. Did you find tranquility here?"

"No."

Booth stopped and turned to face her. "Boy, you sure don't open up easily."

Nova took a long pull on her water and recapped the canteen. "Neither do you."

Their eyes locked. It seemed they both held unspoken truths they dared not utter.

Stalemate.

She marched past Booth. "We're almost there. Let's keep moving."

Ten minutes later they broke through the forest to the homestead, both now breathing hard.

"Oh no." Nova pushed to a run. God, don't let there be anyone inside.

The fire had beaten them here.

Twenty yards ahead, the flames roared through the underbrush, sizzling, cracking, and popping. Orange flames shot up forty to fifty feet on either side of a quaint structure and whipped through the treetops over the metal roof.

Showers of embers rained down. Sparks blew upward and lodged in the branches of a thick black spruce beside the cabin.

She grabbed her radio and called the command desk as she ran up the porch steps. "The head is fanning out at the second homestead. We need a tanker."

"Copy that. Anybody home up there?"

"Checking. We'll save any civilians. Just get that mud up here so we can slow this fire down." She banged on the door. "Hey! Anyone in there? Jude County Smokejumpers! Open up!"

Voices. Footsteps pounded the floor. The doorknob rattled. A bearded man opened the door. He had a muscled arm wrapped around a woman. Probably his wife.

For a second, Nova stared at the couple, so similar to her own parents fifteen years ago. Parents who'd lived in a remote cabin in the mountains. Who'd poured their blood, sweat, and tears into a self-sustaining homestead.

The dirt and ash turned to mud in her mouth, and she swallowed it down. "Get out of the house."

"It's not a house. It's our home." The man lifted his chin. "Tell us what to do so we can save it."

Nova pushed away images from the past. "The fire is moving through here faster than we can keep up. We're doing what we can to contain it, but it's not safe for you to stay. You have to leave. That tree—didn't you get the evacuation notice?"

Stubborn people put their lives at risk thinking they could withstand a fire. And now their obstinacy might get her and Booth killed right along with them. This was her past repeating itself all over the place.

"We were out riding ATVs all morning. Smelled the smoke and headed back."

"If you had an escape, you should've taken it." Nova's words sounded cold. She shifted her weight and tried again. "Look, we need you to evac while you still can. It's worse than you realize."

The man opened the door wider and gaped at the flames consuming the forest less than fifty yards away. "It's...everywhere."

His wife squeezed his arm. "What're we gonna do?"

"I'm Daniel, and this is my wife, Teresa. We don't want to lose our home." He wrung his dry, calloused hands together. "Please tell us what to do."

Daniel's eyes held the same look her father's had when they'd faced the fire. This man might not be a fireman, but he was a hard worker. Like her father had been.

She hadn't been able to save them, but she could help save these people. "You got a chainsaw?"

A few minutes later, Teresa had a hose connected to the well water spigot and was drenching the ground in a line around the home. Daniel used his chainsaw to clear the brush while Booth worked to fell the thick spruce trees threatening to fall on the house.

Nova shoveled mounds of fresh dirt over the spot fires popping up. They were making progress digging a protective line around the property. If things went sideways, they'd run for the small pond on the back side of Daniel's property.

Booth cut the engine on the saw and wiped his

brow. His face was black with sweat and grime. "This little chain saw can't cut this thick one fast enough. I shoulda been through it by now."

Nova's radio crackled. "Nova, we're five minutes to drop. We've got retardant. Clear the area."

"Copy." She wiped two dirty fingers on her shirt and popped them in her mouth. The shrill whistle caught everyone's attention. "Move to the porch! We've got incoming!"

Mud rained down on the roof and filled the air with a salty smell that reminded her of the ocean. The fire-retardant chemicals coated the forest, the grass, and the brush. The humidity level skyrocketed and the air cooled.

Teresa gasped.

Nova glanced at the woman. "It's pretty amazing, right?"

Beyond the older couple, Booth had his eyes on her, not the retardant drop. The darkness from his expression was gone now.

"You're missing the show."

A smile shone in his eyes. "No, I'm not."

She looked at the mess of foam, burnt grass, singed trees, and smoke all around them. So, pretty much her life.

Nothing but disaster and destruction.

Enough of that.

The retardant drop had knocked the flames down and cooled the running fire, but there was still work to do.

She hopped off the porch. "Back to work. Booth and I have a job to do."

Daniel followed. "You need an extra pair of hands?"

The homesteader worked hard, but Nova waffled. "This is dangerous work. Besides the fire, we're constantly at risk of falling limbs. I think you'd better stay here and make that fire line wider. Now that the forest has burned, you won't have much fuel for another wildfire, but you should always be prepared."

"It'd be wise to take a few of the free classes the hotshot crew offers to learn how to protect your home," Booth said.

Teresa hugged Nova. "Thank you. We're so glad you got here when you did."

Nova stood rigid. It was just too weird to be hugged by someone who reminded her of her dead mother.

She let Teresa hold her a beat, then pulled away. "Just, uh, doing our jobs."

Booth and Nova worked all night to pinch off the head, and by early morning, Logan, Vince, Finn, and JoJo had connected the left and right flank lines. They'd contained the fire enough to stop its spread.

Thick gray clouds hovered in the early morning sky and blocked the sunrise. The team had their gear packed and stood in a line waiting.

"You did great work today." Nova scanned the soot- and dirt-covered faces of her crew. "You saved a family. I have new orders from Miles. We're going to split the team. Logan, JoJo, and Vince are gonna meet up with the rest of the Missoula crew working the main fire. My team has twenty-four-hour leave for rest and resupply."

"You heard her." Logan threw his arm forward. "Let's march."

Nova hefted her pack and followed Booth and

Finn toward the clearing where they'd meet the chopper.

Today they'd saved a homestead from a fire not unlike the one that'd killed her parents. But Daniel and Teresa were safe, and Nova could live with that.

The danger wasn't over, though.

Not by far.

Beyond the charred remains of the contained fire, the air thrummed with the distant roar of the real beast. A two-thousand-acre inferno headed west, hungry for the town of Snowhaven.

TWO

Booth's eyes snapped open, and he bolted upright, blankets pooling around his waist. His heart pounded a frantic rhythm against his ribs. Rubbing the grit from his eyes, he tried to get his bearings.

No roaring flames. No pop of gunfire. No screams.

He wasn't working a wildfire, and he wasn't in the explosion with Crispin. He was in his bunk at jump base.

Booth scrubbed a hand down his face, feeling the bristle of beard stubble on his jaw. He'd slept like the dead after working the wind-whipped forest fire all night. Glancing at his watch, he grimaced. Five hours of sleep wasn't nearly enough to recover from the bone-deep exhaustion that came from countless days battling wilderness infernos.

He longed to burrow back under his blanket and catch a few more hours of oblivion, but the sunlight slanting through the room's only window told him it was after noon already. He needed to get a move on. There were things to do in town today—important things. Like trying to find Crispin.

That thirty-second argument under a canoe during the firestorm wasn't going to cut it.

"Go back to your life. I got this," Crispin had said, shouting over the storm's fury.

Like Booth could walk away now.

He'd slapped the water. "Hey, talk to me! We used to be partners. What's going on?"

"Nothing you need to worry about!" Crispin's face was stony as he whispered.

The canoe thrashed in the water. They clung to it while the wind pushed the fire over the lake.

Booth persisted. "If you're in trouble, I can help—"

"I'm trying to keep you out of this," Crispin said.

Booth gritted his teeth and pressed closer to Crispin. "I don't want to stay out of this. Henry sent me here to live this lie, and I've been keeping my head down, thinking Henry must be hiding here." He lowered his voice even more. "But it's been three years, man. I'm losing hope. This is my chance. My one chance to get my life back."

Crispin considered his words. "Listen, Earl has a brother. Floyd. He's dangerous, and he's at the center of this whole thing."

"What whole thing?"

"Just...keep your head on a swivel. If I need you, I'll let you know."

Then the fire had fled and so had Crispin. Vanished after the firestorm without a trace.

Booth couldn't sit idle while his friend faced danger alone. But Crispin had left a thread—Earl's brother Floyd at the center of...what?

If Booth found Crispin first, maybe he could wring some answers from the man. Resolution beckoned—perhaps a chance to finally end this choking lie he lived.

Crispin was out there playing lone wolf. But he was only lying to himself that he didn't need backup. Well, Booth refused to quit now—not when a reckoning approached, promising long-awaited freedom from this fake life he was living.

He'd track down his stubborn friend and watch his six whether Crispin agreed or not.

Earl Blackwell was dead, but the war wasn't over.

With a resigned sigh, Booth levered himself out of bed.

Finn's bunk, opposite his, was already neatly made. The rest of the long, open room was empty, the other jumpers on the fire threatening to overrun a town.

After making his bed with military precision, Booth headed for the restroom. Down the hall near the back stairwell, the shared bathroom smelled of menthol shaving cream. He splashed water on his face and stared at himself in the mirror.

Three years ago, Booth Wilder hadn't existed.

He'd been born under a different name. Born to fight crime, not fires.

Yet here he was. Biding his time until he could fix everything that had gone wrong and finally get back to his real life.

But he was done playing the waiting game.

He was going to find Crispin and find answers.

Booth ran through his hygiene routine and made his way downstairs. Nova's voice echoed down the hallway.

"And this is the manufacturing room, where our smokejumpers use a variety of materials and sewing machines to create the gear we all use." Nova swept her arm toward a doorway. She'd showered and changed into a fresh uniform of green pants, khaki Nomex shirt, and thick boots.

An elderly couple craned their necks to see into the room.

Great. A facility tour.

At least it wasn't his turn. Peopling wasn't his thing.

Nova, on the other hand, was the perfect person to lead informational tours. Born and raised right here in Jude County, she knew all the locals and the best places for tourists to visit. And okay, even he could be drawn in by the natural charisma she didn't seem to know she had.

"Because our equipment and gear are specialized to what we do, every smokejumper, man or woman, learns how to sew. Right, Booth?" She turned and flashed a smile, showing her teeth.

His heart did a little double beat before he realized that smile wasn't for him. Probably, she was putting on a show for the visitors.

Come to think of it, he was pretty sure Nova didn't even like him.

He must have rubbed her the wrong way, because she seemed to always be angry with him for making suggestions out in the field and trying to help her.

Two could play the nice game. He plastered on a wide grin for their guests and pushed his hair out of his eyes. "Yup. I hadn't seen a sewing machine in person before I began my career as a smokejumper. Now I'm an expert."

Finally, she gestured to the elderly couple holding hands. "This is Myron and Jan."

Booth nodded a greeting to the couple. Myron wore loose jeans and a blue flannel. Curly hair bushed out from the sides of his Korean War Veteran ball cap. Jan was a wisp of a woman dressed for running, but he doubted her spindly legs would carry her far. Other than their obvious age, the couple seemed the perfect picture of growing old together.

Too bad Booth would never know what that was like. His love life had fallen apart around the same time his faith had. His ex had ditched him for the nerdy real estate agent that'd sold her a condo. Sure, she'd done the whole *it's not you, it's me* thing. Truth was, she'd gotten close enough to see he was unworthy.

"Myron and Jan are retired. Sold everything to tour America in their RV. They've been all over the country together." Nova's red ponytail bobbed as she spoke.

"I see." Why was she telling him this? He'd probably never see these people again.

Nova rocked back on her heels. "Anyway, show these folks something you've made."

So, what, now she was dragging him into the tour?

"Yeah. Sure, boss." He ducked inside the room and grabbed a pair of yellow pants. "These are our jump pants. They're puncture resistant so if we land in a tree, a stick won't poke through."

Jan gasped. "You land in trees?"

"Not on purpose. Sometimes the terrain is more dangerous than a fire. Trees can fall on us while we're working. Jumps go off course. Branches can catch our parachute canopy and collapse it as we're coming down. Then we're free-falling twenty, thirty, forty feet or more with limbs tearing at our suits. We need all the protection we can get."

He shot a glance at Nova.

Besides their little hang-up yesterday, they'd jumped in dangerous high winds last week to help a camp of teens during what'd turned into a firestorm.

Their boss, Tucker Newman, had been whipped into the tree line and made a hard landing on a roof. Thanks to his suit, instead of being impaled on a branch, the jump boss had broken his leg. He was out the rest of the season, though, which left leadership high and dry.

With a fire on the edge of out of control.

"What're those?" Myron pointed to the supply table that ran down the middle of the room.

Booth left the pants on his sewing table and picked up a yellow-and-red striped bag. He handed it to Myron for inspection. "These bags are for our reserve chutes on the plane. We finished assembling them, and later today, they'll get loaded up with the new chutes."

Jan touched the sagging skin around her neck. "You mean you make your own parachutes too?"

"Yes, ma'am. It's important that we have the skills to manufacture all our own gear, because it's extremely specific to our job. We can't rely on someone else understanding what we do and what we need." Really, he was practically running this tour now.

"Fascinating." Myron studied the bag and handed it to his wife.

"Sewing is a tradition we hand down from year to year." Nova took the bag from Jan and chucked it to

Booth. "All the men around here learn to sew. Isn't that right?"

The bag hit him in the chest, but he caught it. "Yeah. That's right."

"Thanks for the info, Booth." Nova strode across the room to the opposite door, talking to the couple over her shoulder.

He watched, struck by how a woman like Nova could cause his mind to wander to areas he'd rather not explore. Areas that included telling her how sometimes, when he closed his eyes at night, he didn't see the fireball that he'd *thought* had killed his partner. Instead, he saw Nova's fire-red ponytail bouncing as she worked the fire line by his side.

The last person he should be thinking about was a woman who couldn't stand him. She'd been so cold to him, but he had a whole new level of respect for her. If she hadn't thought to leave the crew and go check on the homesteads, that couple would've faced a far different ending.

She cast one last look at him as she disappeared through the doorway. "And that concludes our tour…" Her speech faded out of earshot.

"What are you doing? Keep your head in the game, man," he muttered to himself.

He scratched his ear where dry skin covered a fresh burn. When had that happened? This job. Sheesh. So many mysterious cuts and bruises.

May as well take care of the new reserve chute bags before he headed out. He gathered them into his arms and carried them to the loft upstairs to be packed by someone with way more experience than he had.

Back downstairs, he cut through the ready room,

where the open bay door helped air out the lockers and all their smoke-drenched gear waiting for deployment.

He paused when he saw Finn loading the helicopter. His black hair clung to his head in slick strands, glistening with wetness from either his fresh shower or exertion.

Great. While Booth slept, Finn and Nova had been working. "I'm such a jerk," he muttered.

"You didn't hear it from me," Nova said, stopping to stand beside him. A slight smile tugged at the corners of her mouth.

"Funny." He crossed his arms over his chest. "I didn't mean to sleep so long and leave you guys with all the work."

"It's fine. I can handle things." She nodded to the old couple holding hands, walking to a fifth wheel. "Next time you get to do the tour."

"Me? You're the veteran smokie. If you stuck them with me, I'd probably end up asking them how they manage that gooseneck at their age."

"Seriously? You're a smokejumper and all you can think about is how well they drive their rig?"

No, he'd been thinking about how his cover had been blown by Crispin showing up in Ember. How it might not matter now, because the man who'd died in the fire at Wildlands Academy had been Earl Blackwell. A man willing to kill to get his hands on the missing nuke.

Booth glanced at Nova. He couldn't tell her any of that. She wouldn't believe him if he did. Not after all the Crazy Henry stories he'd been telling around the campfire. "I was thinking how sometimes people aren't what they seem."

There.

He'd left it open to her interpretation.

Nova folded her arms and squared her stance to match his. "Deep. Anyone in particular?"

He cocked his head. "You, for starters. One look at you and some might assume you were too delicate to withstand the types of firestorms we've been through. But they'd be wrong. You're *so* not fragile. I've seen the real fire blaze in your eyes working the fire line, shoulder to shoulder with men twice your size."

Nova removed her long-sleeved Nomex shirt and tied it around her waist. The worn blue undershirt had a faded Jude County Smokejumpers logo on it. "What can I say? This job is in my blood."

He watched Myron open the passenger door for Jan. Before she got in, she stretched up on her tiptoes and kissed her husband.

Real life.

Booth looked at his dirty boots. Rubbed the toe in the gravel. Someone else's real life—not his.

"So, what about you?" Nova asked. "Where'd you come from?"

"That's...a story for another time." He lifted his chin to Jan, headed right for them. "Forget to buy your Jude County Smokejumpers sweatshirt in the gift shop?"

The old woman smiled. "No, honey. Thought I better use the ladies' room before we get back on the road."

"Let me show you. I know a shortcut." Nova waved for Jan to follow, then paused. "Booth, could you grab a few first aid kits and run them to Finn?"

Oh, she was asking now? "Happy to."

Before he left, maybe he could make a few calls. See if anyone working down at the Hotline had seen a man matching Crispin's description.

His phone was dead. Great. He'd crashed so hard last night he hadn't charged it. There was a charger in his pickup, and he'd have to plug it in on his way to Ember.

Right after he did the first aid kits.

In the supply room, Booth found the kits, but they hadn't been packed with supplies. He filled each one with all the supplies and marked them on the inventory sheet, noting they needed more gauze and antibacterial ointment—which he should probably put on the small burns he'd received yesterday.

He stacked all three tool-kit-sized boxes and rested his chin on the top one. He grabbed the doorknob.

Locked.

Weird. This door locked from the inside.

Booth peered around the kits and tried the handle. Jerked harder.

The door wasn't locked, but it was stuck.

And now he was trapped.

Now was as good a time as any to march next door to Miles's office and have the conversation. The one where she stepped up and offered to lead the team in Tucker's stead.

But first, she had to do her job. The part where she provided hospitality to locals and visitors alike.

She led Jan through the halls and cut through the

back, where they didn't take the tour groups. This area had their lounge. Their personal space.

The supply room door creaked, and Nova stole a glance at Booth ambling in.

Man, there had to be more going on in his head than make-believe stories about spies and stolen nukes. Right?

No matter how hard Nova tried, she couldn't figure out Booth Wilder. There was a secret hidden behind his kind eyes. A secret she couldn't penetrate.

Maybe he'd ditched a wife and kids. Or was on the run from the law.

Nah. Booth might be hiding something, but it was no secret he was a good man. Had trouble listening to her orders without question, but then, she hadn't been named crew chief yet either. But on and off the fire, nothing seemed to ruffle his feathers, and Nova found herself calmer just being near him.

Maddening.

"Sure is quiet around here. Where is everyone?" Jan's words interrupted Nova's whirlwind thoughts.

"We've got a pretty big fire burning, so we have teams out trying to control it. There's six of us here. You met Booth, but the other four are out in the airplane hangar, repacking cargo for the next deployment."

Jan paused and studied the photos mounted on plaques lining the hall. "Are these the rest of your crew?"

"This is the memorial wall." Nova's eyes drifted down the line of photos to the one she knew best. "Smokejumpers killed in the line of duty."

"Wow. So many." Jan stopped and looked at Nova with soft eyes. "I hope you don't mind me asking, but what makes a pretty, young girl like you decide to do such a dangerous job?"

Nova took a few steps, stopping in front of a photo. She slid her fingers over the gold nameplate. "This is my uncle Jock." She gestured to the line of photos extending past him. "These guys were all killed when they were overrun by a fire. Good people die in wildfires. I lost my own parents in one." She paused. Swallowed. Shrugged. "The way I see it, I didn't have a choice. It's my legacy. I'll never find peace in this world as long as fires are raging."

"I bet your uncle and your parents would be proud of you."

"Thanks. I'm determined to live up to my uncle Jock's legacy and one day be crew chief." And that day would come soon if she played her cards right.

Nova pointed out the main exit doors and left Jan in the ladies' room.

Back in the memorial hallway, she paused at Jock's picture. Touched her fingers to her lips and pressed them to the photo.

It was time to talk to Miles.

She retraced her steps to the ready room and twisted the doorknob. It worked, but the door wouldn't budge. She bumped it with her shoulder. Stuck.

Why was the door even shut? They always kept it open for callouts.

She turned on her heel and strode to the supply room. Her right hand grabbed the knob. "Booth, why'd you lock the—"

The door wouldn't budge. She slid her phone from her pocket and dialed Booth. Straight to voicemail.

"You can't lock the doors around here." She knocked her knuckles on the metal frame. "Open up."

"What are you talking about? I wasn't the one who locked the door." The knob rattled and turned from the other side. "Let me out."

"Just unlock it."

"I'm telling you, it's not locked. It's stuck."

"I tried the ready room door and it was stuck too." Nova's pulse kicked up. "This is too weird."

A loud thud came from the other side, followed by a low grunt. Nova flinched. Booth wasn't messing around.

"Nope, won't budge. I'm locked in tight," he said through the door. "Look around the casing out there. Do you see anything stuck?"

Nova ran her eyes around the edge. "Yeah. It looks like something's wedged in there and broken off. A piece of wood maybe."

"Listen to me." Booth's voice had the firmness of an officer giving an order. "Get out! You need to find a way out of the building! Now!"

Goosebumps raced up Nova's arms. She could picture the blackened face and smell the woodsy char from the fire that had taken Earl's life. She inhaled a deep breath.

Wait.

Why could she smell it right now?

This wasn't a nostalgic moment. Nova whirled. Smoke wafted down the hall. "Booth, I see smoke. There's a fire. The building is on fire."

"Get out of the building right now!"

Booth couldn't see her, but she was already shaking her head. "No. No way. I'm not leaving you trapped in there."

A smoke detector let loose an ear-piercing shriek. Nova flinched. A second alarm blared. One after another, the daisy-chained smoke detectors triggered. The entire building had one screaming from every room.

"Nova? Can you hear me?"

She covered her other ear. "Barely."

"I can knock the pins out of the hinges on this side. I've got gear in here. Go! I'll be right behind you."

"Okay! I'm leaving, but you better meet me outside in two minutes, and that's an order." One she prayed he'd take for once.

Somewhere in the building, there was a loud crash. A woman screamed.

Nova sucked in a breath. "Jan! She must still be in the restroom."

"Go! Help her!"

Nova pulled her Nomex shirt on over her T-shirt. Thick black smoke filled the hallway. She yanked the fire extinguisher off the wall and raced for the ladies' room.

"Jan! It's Nova. I'm coming to you! Stay where you are if you can!"

Nova shouldered through the bathroom door, heart pounding. She wasn't a city firefighter. She fought blazes in forests, not bathrooms.

Smoke plumed through the vents, but there wasn't an active fire.

"Jan are you in here?" The stall doors were open, but Nova checked them anyway.

"Help! Help me!" Jan coughed. "I'm trapped!"

Okay, not in the bathroom. In the lobby?

Nova dashed out of the restroom and ran to the expansive lobby. A wall of heat pressed into her face. Flames made a hot run up the walls, headed for the ceiling. Fiery tendrils spread along the baseboards, searching for more oxygen and fuel to feed itself.

"Jan, it's Nova! I'm in the lobby. Where are you?"

She listened for the woman, but all she heard was the popping and crackling roar of destruction. Great clouds of thick smoke boiled up and stung her eyes.

Zero visibility.

She shrugged the fire extinguisher up on one hip and used her free arm to pat her pockets for a flashlight. Blast. She'd left it in her personal gear bag at her locker.

Okay, think.

She used the flashlight app on her phone to look around. Straight ahead, a red exit sign hung over the glass doors that she could barely see through the smoky haze. To the left was the reception desk no one ever used. The big wooden unit had nearly been consumed by flames at this point.

The wide doorway of the visitors' center led into the smokejumper museum, where the fire stayed minor. For now.

"Jan! Tell me where you are so I can—" Ash thickened her tongue and she coughed.

Distant voices shouted commands from somewhere outside. Help was coming, but if she didn't stop the fire from spreading, it would come too late.

Nova pocketed her phone and pulled the safety pin on the extinguisher. She squinted against the swirling smoke and backed into the exhibit room.

White foam hissed from the fire extinguisher's nozzle as she doused the flames around the museum doorway in a sweeping arc. She covered the floor, wall, ceiling. The expanding cloud of fire retardant smothered the blaze, buying them precious seconds.

There was a loud splintering sound over her head.

The ceiling caved.

Nova scrambled back a second before debris and fire rained down on her head. A flashover had started. The fire in the ceiling ate its way through to the second floor of the building. Any minute now, everything could collapse on top of her. Help wouldn't be able to get to them in time.

Nova emptied the fire extinguisher on the pile of rubble and tossed the spent canister aside. She turned. Faced the darkened room.

Coils of smoke snaked around the Z-shaped museum walls. Years of memorabilia, artifacts, and firefighting collectibles. Jock's old uniform. All massacred now by the same element they'd valiantly fought for years.

She spotted a hard lump on the floor in front of the display. Unmoving.

Images of Jan up on her tiptoes and kissing her husband beside their rig rolled through her mind.

No. No. No.

Not another beautiful marriage destroyed by fire.

Nova rushed to the figure and dropped to her knees. At least Jan had been smart enough to cover herself with an old fire coat.

Nova grabbed her by the shoulders. Rigid shoulders.

Oh no. She rolled the body over and gasped. Gave herself a little jump scare and choked. Coughed.

Her eyes stung with tears. Not Jan. Not Jan! A stupid mannequin! A dummy dressed like a smokejumper from the forties.

So much for being a hero.

Jan had to be here somewhere. She tugged the fire jacket off the fiberglass figure and tossed it around her shoulders.

Now, stay low. Limit smoke inhalation. Find Jan. Get the heck outta here.

Smoldering museum relics crumbled under her boots as she crept through the sweltering air. A few feet away, she saw another lump. Familiar puffs of gray hair peeked out.

"Jan! Jan, are you okay?" Hot smoke burned her raw throat.

Nova fell to her knees beside the unconscious older woman and assessed her condition. Thready pulse. Shallow breaths. Legs pinned by a ten-foot-long birch log used in a display. The thing had to weigh close to seven hundred pounds.

The ceiling splintered with a thunderous crack.

She threw herself over Jan as a desk from the second-floor offices crashed down beside them, barely missing them. The desk teetered on two legs, then fell against the wall.

They had to get out of here before the whole death trap collapsed.

She pulled the ancient turnout coat off her shoulders and draped it over Jan. Crawled a few feet away and grabbed an old leather oxygen mask and slipped it over her head.

Lord, let this antiquated thing work. She breathed in stale, leathery air. If nothing else, the dusty goggles would keep the smoke out of her eyes.

"Hang on. I'll get this thing off you."

She squatted and tried to lift the massive log. It was too hot and too heavy. Ugh, she needed her gloves.

Give me a lever long enough and I'll move the world…

The quote her father had often used rolled through her mind.

Yes, she needed a lever! She scanned the room for something, anything that would work, but came up short.

It didn't matter.

She could do this.

She could prevent Jan from burning. Give the EMTs the best chance to save her.

She braced her hands on the burning floorboards and her boots against the smoldering log. With all her leg strength, she heaved. It didn't move.

Red hot embers and ash fell on Jan.

New plan. She scurried around the woman, grabbed her under both arms, and pulled. Debris rained down and pelted her. Small stabs of pain pricked her skin where the fire burned holes through her shirt as she worked to free the woman.

The shouts outside grew louder. There was a booming thud. Another. Another.

Sounds of wood splintering. Shards of wood flying.

She turned. Tried to see through the goggles clouded by age.

A hulking shadow stormed through the fire, heading right toward them, marching over broken two-by-fours and blazing maps of the same Kootenai National Forest where she battled wildfires.

A hero coming through the flames to save her.

The very last hero that she wanted. But the one she probably needed.

This time.

THREE

GREAT, HIS WORST FEAR. BEING TRAPPED IN A house fire. At least out in the wilderness he had options. He could run.

No running now. He'd spent the better part of five minutes driving the pins out of the hinges only to go from the frying pan into the fire.

Smoke filled the hallway as he fought upstream through a pit of swirling gray haze, searching for Jan and Nova.

Crackling and popping sounds came from every direction. The walls beside him. The floor beneath him. The ceiling over him.

Yep, worse than any wildfire.

"Nova! Where are you?" Booth shouted into the smoke-filled hallway. "Help is coming. Finn's trying to find a safe way in." A way that wouldn't send the whole building crashing in on them.

He slammed into the ladies' room. Nothing here.

"Nova!"

He continued down the hall and tried a side exit. No dice. Someone had jammed all the doors on purpose.

Whoever had done this had set fires at every exit and doused the place with gasoline. The local fire department was en route—he'd called them the second he'd escaped—but they were miles away. Jump base had tools and equipment for wildfires, not buildings.

Booth radioed Finn. "I can't find them anywhere. They have to be in the museum. It's the only place I haven't checked."

"Ten-four," Finn said. "Can you get in there?"

"Hang on." Booth ran through the smoke-filled lobby to the history room and paused at the entrance. "It's fully engulfed, but yes."

"Good. I'll grab my saw and cut an exit hole in the southwest corner. I don't see any fire or smoke there...yet," Finn added. "It'll be a miracle if my blade can cut through the metal siding without breaking a chain, but just get there."

"I'll make it happen." He'd find Nova and Jan, get them to the spot, and let God handle the miracle.

Booth pressed a sleeve over his nose and jumped through the pile of burning rubble. He scanned the room.

Where are you, Wildfire Girl?...C'mon, give me a sign.

There! Through curtains of black smoke, he spotted her red hair. She was crouched beside a lump on the floor, kicking at a log three times the diameter of a telephone pole.

And was she...? Yeah, she was wearing one of those old bug-eyed gas masks from the early days of firefighting. He'd laugh if the situation weren't dire.

He closed the expanse, crushing charred remnants of museum artifacts underfoot. "Nova!"

Her head twitched an acknowledgment, but Nova

didn't stop driving her boot into the wood. "Give me a hand!"

One of the logs used to mimic the trees smokejumpers and hotshots felled had come loose from the wall anchors and fallen, pinning Jan's legs.

Blood trickled from a small cut on the older woman's cheek.

She wasn't moving.

For one heart-stopping instant, he feared the worst. Then the slow rise and fall of Jan's ribcage eased his clenching gut.

Not dead. Unconscious.

Was kicking the thing really the right way to help Jan?

He gripped Nova's shoulder and gave her a firm shake. She wrenched to look at him. "Hey, take a breath real quick. We'll get her free."

She gave one sharp shake of her head. "No. I can't…I can't…Just help. We've gotta get this off her now!"

Nova was right. Bulging pipes skewered the flaming walls on every side, destabilized further by each crashing ceiling section bringing down the building overhead. They were living on borrowed time. Minutes at best.

"I know. We can do this. We'll lift it together. Here, take my gloves." He pulled one off.

"No, you'll need them."

"One is better than none. Take it!"

She snatched the glove and tugged it over her hand. "Just help me, will you!"

He joined Nova on the floor and added his strength to hers. Together, they heaved. His muscles quivered as they fought for every ounce of power he possessed.

The blasted thing refused to budge.

Time for a new plan.

"This won't work. We need a pry bar." Booth scanned the wreckage.

Biting back coughs, he picked his way across the room and grabbed a sturdy piece of wood. "I'll lever it up, you grab Jan."

Nova hesitated a beat, brow furrowed. Then she nodded. "Got it. Good idea."

Booth drove the board under the log and looked to Nova. "Easy does it. We need to lift just enough for you to do your thing."

"On three." Nova stood over Jan and gripped the woman under the arms. "One, two, three!"

Booth applied pressure. The wood he used as a lever creaked and groaned. The log lifted an inch.

"Little more...c'mon," Nova rasped.

He gritted his teeth and drove his weight harder against the lever.

"Al...most..." Nova slid Jan a few inches and repositioned to wrap her hands around Jan's waist.

Booth groaned and put all his muscle into adding pressure. A long split zigzagged across the lever. "Hurry! It won't hold much longer!"

"I've...got...her." With one last pull, Nova shimmied Jan free.

The board snapped under Booth's hands, and the log crashed to the floor, sending flaming sparks crackling upward.

Panting, they stared at each other for a beat. Nova's big eyes blinked behind the goggles.

"We're not—" Coughs wracked Booth's body, and

he leaned over to spit ash out of his mouth. "—out of the woods yet."

A resounding boom announced another section of ceiling caving in. Tornadoes of scalding embers swirled around Booth's head. He coughed again, swallowing a lungful of soot.

"Booth…? You still…in one piece…?" Nova choked out the words.

"I'm…fine." He scrambled over to lift Jan. The woman's head lolled as he lifted her over his shoulder, careful of her legs.

"Here." Nova tossed the turnout coat that had fallen back over Jan.

"Follow me." He carried Jan deeper into the museum to a far corner, tromping over burning debris.

Daylight peeked through the outline of a small rectangle where Finn had cut a makeshift door in the wall. Booth drove his boot into the plaster. It buckled.

Nova touched his shoulder. "I got it." She kicked the remaining Sheetrock out from between the studs.

From the other side, Booth heard shouting.

"Stand back and I'll cut the studs," Finn yelled. The chainsaw growled to life and chewed through the wood. Two cuts at the top and two at the bottom. Hands reached in and yanked out the section of boards. "Okay, you're clear!"

Nova helped Booth pass Jan through the small opening.

"Watch her legs," Nova said.

Booth stepped back. "Your turn."

Nova shook her head and took a step to the side. "You first."

This was no time for arguing, and it wouldn't do

any good anyway. Nova was too headstrong. "See you on the other side."

He crawled through the hole and felt hands grabbing him under the arms, helping him up. Booth sucked in clean air and coughed.

Then Nova was by his side, coughing right along with him. She ripped off her mask and dropped it to the ground.

Local firefighters had arrived and were dousing the building with water. An ambulance screamed to a stop on the asphalt, and two men jumped out. One ran to get his gear. The other headed for where Finn had laid Jan on the ground.

Still coughing, Nova gave the paramedic a rundown. "Her name is Jan. She was unconscious when I found her in the fire. One of those big tree logs in the museum fell on her legs. Last I checked, she was breathing. Pulse steady. Both slow."

"Thanks, we've got her." The paramedic knelt and went to work. "Do you know this woman's medical history?"

Booth searched the crowd. The fire captain was with Miles, shouting over the roar of water now streaming out of hoses. A few other faces he didn't recognize stood around, arms folded. Hotshots probably. He spotted Myron shuffling toward them. "That's her husband right there."

The second paramedic said, "We can take it from here."

Behind Myron, a burly man with a shaved head and bushy beard stood alone near the airplane hangar. He wore baggy jeans, a concert T-shirt, and a black leather vest. Black wraparound sunglasses obscured his eyes. Smoke drifted from the tip of the cigarette between his first two fingers.

Definitely not meant to be here.

They made eye contact. The man stuck the cigarette between his lips. Inhaled a long drag, then flicked the still burning stub into the grass.

Booth's throat tightened. He wasn't just out here on a smoke break. There was nothing innocent about the man or the cigarette.

I know you.

A familiarity tugged at Booth's memory, like an invisible string stretching to connect the dots. If the guy would take off those shades, let Booth see his eyes, maybe he could figure it out.

Shades fished in his pocket and pulled out something small and red. A lighter. He leaned against the hangar and worked his thumb over it, lighting a small flame and letting it die. Again and again, with a big stupid grin on his face.

Clearly Shades knew something Booth didn't. Why not go ask what was so funny?

He strode across the parking lot on a mission. Shades pushed off the aluminum building and disappeared around the corner.

Booth picked up his pace and jogged the last few yards. The stink of cigarettes lingered along with another distinctive odor. Gasoline.

This guy had set the fire.

The fire that'd almost killed Jan. And Nova.

Booth clenched his fists and rounded the corner in time to catch a blur coming.

He ducked.

The object sailed inches above his head. He

bounced up to see Shades holding a tire iron. The big stupid grin had transformed into a sinister smirk.

Booth rocked back on his heels, fists up. "Who sent you?"

"Don't matter. Money's money." Shades turned the tire iron over in his hand.

All the saliva in Booth's mouth dried up.

Shades was some sort of assassin. One who didn't care about collateral damage.

Nova rounded the corner and gasped.

In the split second Booth took to steal a glance, Shades made his move.

He swung the bar like a baseball bat aimed at Booth's head.

Nova's brain took its sweet time comprehending what her eyes were seeing.

A fire had threatened her life not ten minutes ago, and now Booth was facing off with this…this *tank* swinging a tire iron. "Booth! Watch out!"

Booth sidestepped at the last second.

Iron clanged against the hangar. A shower of sparks burst from metal against metal.

A blow that could have cracked his skull. Was he crazy? Why was Booth fighting with this maniac? He should just stand down.

"Wait!" Booth held up a hand. "Wait. Tell me who paid you."

"Ain't nobody payin' till you're dead." The tank of a man lunged forward, bar raised to strike again.

Booth dodged. "I can pay more."

Tank swung the bar up again. Tossed it to his left hand, then back to his right. "So can they."

"Booth? What's he talking about?" She glanced at Tank. "Did someone pay you to start that fire?"

"Stay out of this, Nova." Booth took a step toward Tank. "Go. Grab the sheriff. This guy's the arsonist."

Stay out of it? This was absurd. "C'mon, break it up! Booth, just walk away."

"Nova, just get out—"

Tank took another swing.

Booth did some sort of fancy maneuver where he leaned back and twisted his shoulders away. The blow breezed over his head. He came back up and drove his fist into the paunch of Tank's stomach.

Those were some pretty good fighting moves for a smokejumper.

"I'm telling you for the last time, go!"

Nova flinched at his tone and stepped a few feet back. She needed a plan. One that didn't include Booth getting killed or her leaving him.

She looked all around. They were two hundred yards away from the parking lot, where first responders worked to save the jump base. She wasn't sure anyone would hear her shouting for help over the blast of fire hoses and equipment.

Nova felt her right pocket for her phone. Then her left. Found it and unlocked the screen. "Hey, you. Big guy. Smile." She snapped a photo of Tank. "This is all the sheriff needs—"

Tank charged forward and hooked a hard strike. The phone flew out of her hand and exploded with a crunch of glass and metal. Nova yelped. Pain bloomed in her empty hand.

Tank rounded the iron over his head for another go.

Booth dove in front of her. The bar connected with his upper arm with a soft thud.

Nova sucked air between her teeth, but Booth didn't seem fazed by the blow. He whirled and threw a hard punch to Tank's temple. The sunglasses covering his eyes flew off and landed in the grass.

Tank roared and came at Booth wild. Fists flailing. Feet kicking.

Booth deflected his strikes and jabbed the biker in the stomach. Nova silently cheered when Booth landed another blow, this time to the biker's ribs, but the guy countered with an elbow to Booth's face.

Both men circled each other, panting hard. A bit of blood trickled from the corner of Booth's mouth before he wiped it with the back of his hand.

Tank was turning out to be just as dangerous as the nickname she'd given him. And what good was she? An unarmed smokejumper, currently thinking about running.

In fact, she backed up. Two steps. Three. Her heel caught on something hard and she tripped. Fell flat on her rear, hands splayed out behind her. She blinked.

Booth took half a step toward her. "Are you—"

Tank charged.

Booth turned sideways. Slapped a hand on the man's neck while the other hand grabbed the back of his pants. Booth heaved him forward.

Tank stumbled but planted a hand on the grass and pushed himself off.

His bald head came up, and he spun to face Booth. Sniffed. Spat on the ground. "You're a dead man." He pointed the tire iron at Nova. "You and your little girlfriend too."

"Girlfriend? I'm not his girlfriend." Apparently that was the thing to snap her out of her paralysis. Although, she might've been focusing on the wrong thing. "What do you want with us anyway? We're just smokejumpers."

Her eyes darted back to Tank. He could've killed Jan. Maybe he had. And what if the crew had been in the building? "There were people inside, and you set the building on fire?"

Tank sneered. "That's right, sweetie pie."

"Don't talk to her." Booth's head twitched to look at her. "Please. Go."

She caught the pleading in his eyes but couldn't walk away. He hadn't left her in the fire, and she wasn't about to leave him either.

Tank roared and lunged. He hit Booth in a hard tackle.

Nova gasped.

The men fell to the ground with Tank's massive form covering Booth. Tank had the tire iron in both hands and under Booth's chin. They grunted and growled, each trying to get the upper hand.

Booth grasped the bar and pushed back, his face turning red.

"Booth!" Nova sucked in a breath. Got a running start. Hauled her right leg back and kicked. Her boot connected with Tank's ribs.

Air exploded from Tank, and he rolled over onto the grass, gasping for breath.

Booth pushed Tank off his legs and struggled to his feet. The iron dangled from his hand. Booth coughed and rubbed the red spot at his throat.

Behind her, Tank called her a few choice names, one of which she found pretty insulting. She turned to say so, but Booth stepped in front of her.

Tank was on his feet, shoulders hunched. There was a metallic click. Nova saw the silver blade jump out of the knife handle clutched in his meaty hand.

"I'm going to cut your pretty little face up for that, missy."

Nova's stomach dropped to the floor. This was serious.

Booth took two steps toward him. "You touch her and it's the last thing you'll do."

"Watch out!" she yelled.

Tank dove at Booth, but Booth was a step ahead. He caught Tank's wrists in his palms and drove the man's hands up. "Get outta here, Nova!"

Booth had his hands wrapped around the knife. Tank swore and brought his knee up fast and hard. Booth folded in half and released his hold on the weapon.

"That's what I thought." Tank strode toward Nova and pointed the knife at her. "Your turn."

Nova froze. Her mouth fell open. Every self-defense situation she'd ever trained for fell out of her head.

Tank took another step. Booth hit him from behind. This time, Tank didn't go down. He pivoted and swung the knife in a wide arc. Booth jumped back and hit Tank's wrist using both palms in a fast X motion that Nova finally remembered learning. The knife flew out of Tank's hand. Booth hit him with a surprise uppercut followed by a left to the nose.

Tank staggered. He spat a wad of blood at Booth's feet. "This ain't over, *kozel*!" He turned and ran.

Booth started to go after him, but Nova grabbed his arm. "Come on, we need to tell the police about this guy so they can catch him."

He pulled his arm away and shook his head. "That's what I've been telling you to do this whole time!"

"Well, excuse me. I didn't want to leave you fighting some crazy dude—who had a *knife* by the way."

"Yes. He had a *knife*. A knife, Nova. You could've been hurt."

"So could you!" Her voice was ratcheting up, but she didn't do anything to stop it. "That's why I said to walk away. You're not a cop, Booth. Catching that guy is not your job. You should've told the police and let *them* do their jobs."

Booth's jaw tightened. "I told *you* to get the police."

She took a step closer. "And I told you I wanted to stay. That's my right. You're not the boss of me."

"Yeah, I'm well aware. But can't you just listen to someone, even if they're not the boss?" His eyes stabbed her with an angry glare. "I really don't get you sometimes."

Booth turned and sprinted in the direction of Tank.

And she just stood there with the sting of his words hot on her face.

After he'd disappeared around the corner, Nova searched for her phone in the grass.

She was having trouble wrapping her head around why Booth felt like it was his responsibility to go after that guy. From what little she'd heard, Tank wasn't a random arsonist playing with fire. He'd come to jump base looking for Booth.

He'd set his sights on killing him.

Leaving her with one big question.

Who was Booth really?

FOUR

BOOTH STOOD THERE WATCHING THE ARSONIST disappear into the mountains on a dirt bike. He'd lost him. Lost his chance to find answers.

Every muscle itched to slam his fist into the side of the airplane hangar, but he didn't. He shouldn't have wasted so much time arguing with Nova when it hadn't done any good anyway. All it'd done was give the arsonist more time to make his escape.

Booth sighed, running a hand through his hair. There was nothing to do now except go back and explain everything to the police.

Trudging back across the parking lot, Booth spotted Miles, Finn, and Nova talking in a circle near the charred museum. As he approached, Nova's gaze flicked to him before she crossed her arms and stared at her feet.

How much had she told them?

"There you are," Miles said, waving him into the circle. "We were just discussing the fire and how it was clearly arson. Any ideas about who was behind this?"

Booth met Nova's fixed stare. "Not exactly."

In a short, concise way, he explained his confrontation with the bald man who had admitted to starting the fire. "I tried to catch him, but he escaped on a dirt bike he had stashed behind the hangar. I'm sorry I couldn't stop him."

Miles clapped a hand on Booth's shoulder. "Nothing to apologize for. If it wasn't for your quick thinking and bravery, that woman could have died in there. We all owe you, Nova, and Finn a huge debt for saving her life."

Miles's phone rang, and he checked the screen. "I'll be in the command center," he whispered, walking away with his phone to his ear.

Booth stared at what used to be the front of jump base. "This is worse than I thought."

Insulation and burnt wood littered the parking lot. The main entrance, visitors' center, museum, and their brand-new sleeping quarters, added as a second level, lay in one big pile of charred, wet rubble.

His eyes drifted to the exit hole Finn had cut. If they hadn't escaped, their bodies would have been somewhere under the debris.

Exactly what the arsonist had intended.

"We're definitely going to need a new place to live," Nova said.

Booth studied Nova. She still hadn't looked at him, and now her eyes stayed fixed on the blackened and charred remnants of the building.

He needed to touch base with his partner, Crispin, and see if his old friend knew why this had happened. No way could it be a coincidence, trapping him inside and trying to kill him.

It had to mean Booth was getting close to something.

He raked a hand through his sticky hair. "And to think I was looking forward to a hot shower."

"I can hit you with the fire hose." Finn looked Booth up and down. "Come to think of it, that might be the only way to get that muck off you."

Booth nodded to the remnants of jump base. "What's the situation?"

Finn exhaled a deep breath. "The fire got between the floors. The offices and sleeping quarters caved in, but the ready room and most of our gear is unharmed."

"I guess Nova's right," Booth said. "We can't stay here. It's not safe. Besides, it's a crime scene."

Nova nodded. "So where do we go?"

"Sophie talked with Miles and suggested campin' out at her ranch," Finn said. "She has a garage where we can set up the speed racks, and you can store cargo in the barn with the horses. Fire management agreed, and Logan, Vince, Eric, and JoJo are heading back to help make the move."

"I guess it's a bath in the horse trough, then." Booth shot a look to Nova. "Should work. What do you think, Boss Lady?"

"We'd be with the horses?" Nova shifted her weight.

Finn chuckled. "Not with them, but they do live on the ranch."

"Is Sheriff Hutchinson still around?" Booth searched the faces but didn't see him.

"Just got here a few minutes ago. He's in the hangar." Finn jerked his chin in that direction.

"Thanks." Booth took a step, but Nova stopped him.

"I'm coming with you." Her face was smeared

with layers of soot and ash. Remnants of her willingness to risk her life and everything she had just to save lives.

"No." The last thing he wanted was her overhearing answers to difficult questions.

Her eyebrows went up. "I was there. And it wasn't a request. C'mon."

Sheriff Hutchinson paced near the entrance, phone to his ear. Booth waited until he finished his call before he approached. "Hey, Sheriff. I'm Booth Wilder, and this is Nova Burns."

"Just the two I needed to see." He nodded to Nova. "You were in the visitors' center, right?"

"Yes, sir," Nova said.

He hooked a thumb on his duty belt. "What's your take on the fire?"

"Arson," she said.

"You seem certain."

Nova nodded. "I know fire. We had spot fires at every exit, and someone had jammed the doors so we couldn't escape."

"And we had a run-in with the arsonist," Booth interjected.

"That so?" The sheriff crooked a finger. "I think you two better come with me."

For the next few hours, Booth sat with Nova, reliving the fire and recounting their run-in with the arsonist to the sheriff and a deputy who jotted down notes.

By the time they'd finished, their crew had made it back and loaded the speed racks and gear on the plane. Aria was doing the preflight checks, ready to fly everything over to Sophie's so they could unload before sunset.

"Everyone in the vans!" Logan shouted. "We're pulling out in five."

Booth slept on the hour-long drive to Sunflower Ranch and woke when the van hit the pothole-filled driveway. They pulled up to the house not far from where Aria had her plane on the ground.

He was one of the last to climb out of the van and paused to stretch. His knees ached, and his lower back did a little snap, crackle, pop.

The smell of burning charcoal and grilled meat wafted from a barbecue, where Sophie stood turning patties. His stomach rumbled, but the jerky and power bar he'd eaten earlier would have to hold a little while longer.

Each smokejumper worked a three-day shift with one day off during fire season, but they were on call even on their day off. They'd need to get the equipment set up to go at a moment's notice.

"All right," Nova shouted. "Now the real work begins. Let's get this plane unloaded."

Finn moaned. "I need sustenance."

Booth tossed a granola bar, and Finn caught it between his palms. "Sooner we get done, the sooner we can eat a real meal."

Nova rounded the corner, attempting to drag a rack all by herself.

Booth set his water down and jogged over. "Here, let me help."

"I think I got it." Sweat dripped from the red curls plastered to Nova's forehead and cut streaks through the black ash and grime on her face. Her boot caught a rock and she stumbled.

And that was just enough. He walked over and picked up the other end of the rack. Together, they carried it to the entrance of the barn and handed it off to Vince and Eric.

Nova looked at him, this time with softness in her eyes. "Thanks."

"You don't have to do everything alone." He smiled and headed back to the plane for another load.

Aria dropped a box on the stack and pushed out a breath. "You're gettin' under her skin, ya know?" She pulled her ball cap off and held the bill between her teeth while she gathered her hair off her neck.

Booth walked up the ramp. "Who?"

"Nova. She doesn't ask for help easily."

"Ever," he corrected.

Aria tugged her hat back on and leaned on the stack of boxes. "It's not easy to lose your parents. Believe me, I know. You tend to erect walls. Mostly I figure only someone who's worth it will take the time to chip away and see who's really inside."

He studied Aria. Saw the pain in her eyes. "You?"

She picked at a piece of tape. "Yeah. Died in Sri Lanka."

Booth gave her space to get the words out.

"My parents were missionaries. They thought they were doing God's work, but you know what they called the tsunami?"

"An act of God?"

Aria turned and grabbed another box. Carried it to the ramp and started a new stack. "Exactly." She set the box down hard. "So trust me when I say that Nova has reasons for her walls. It's up to you to decide if you want to see what's behind them."

For a moment yesterday, as they were walking, he'd thought maybe he had. And again after he'd watched her try so hard to save the homestead. But even now, as he cast a look at her restacking supplies…she seemed so driven. Alone, yes, but driven.

Maybe people could say the same about him.

Booth picked up the stack of boxes. He stopped at the bottom of the ramp and turned. "Hey, Aria?"

She looked up from her clipboard.

"Thanks for the tip."

"Just…be careful with my friend."

Booth nodded and went back to work.

Over the top of his load, he caught sight of Nova. She was bent over, running the water hose over her head. When she stood, she flung her long red hair back, sending water spraying in an arc.

Oh yeah. She was under his skin all right.

Especially when Nova wrung the water out of her hair, noticed him, and smiled.

He smiled back, then turned away. Because, not for the first time, the sight of her stopped him, made him take a breath. Even all sooted up, she had a raw beauty, but most of the time, her cool demeanor kept all those thoughts on a low simmer.

But she'd smiled at him when she'd thanked him, and…yeah, he liked the mystery behind her. Except… one day he'd have to choose between trying to pull back her layers and walking back into his old life.

No, he was only biding his time here, so it wasn't like any of this was real. Nova and what could be was just a wish. A dream he couldn't have.

At least, not with an assassin out there possessing a hit order with his name on it.

Nova stared at the dancing flames in the campfire, exhausted beyond belief. If she weren't so hungry, she'd crawl into her tent and pass out. Maybe a shower first. But it was the banter and laughs from the crew she knew were equally tired that kept her sitting around the fire, listening to the stories fresh off the line.

She finished her hamburger and tossed the napkin in the fire. It shriveled and disappeared in a second.

In the flames, faces appeared—Daniel's, which then morphed into her father's. She was thankful for the image, because some days she worried she might forget what he looked like.

The wildfire at the homestead had dredged up painful memories, but with her help, the outcome had been very different.

A bottle appeared out of the corner of her eye, and she turned to see Booth. "Ice-cold root beer. Sophie had two, so I threw a few elbows and snagged one for you."

"Oh man. I was craving sugar." She took the bottle. Twisted off the cap. Tossed it into the fire. Tipped her head back and took a long pull. The sweetness instantly energized her. "Oh man, that's the stuff."

"What? Nothing for me? I thought I was your favorite." Finn threw up his arms.

Booth sat on the upturned log beside her, his shoulder brushing hers. "You're everybody's favorite, Finn." Booth chuckled.

Nova sipped her soda and tried not to smile at Booth. She was still a little cranky about the way he'd talked to her after the fight, but then, she hadn't exactly been a peach herself.

From the day he'd arrived, Booth had intrigued her, but he was always so buttoned up. Then yesterday, during their walk, he'd given her a glimpse beneath the surface. He was a thinker. Dependable.

And no, she hadn't needed any help with the rack, but the fact he'd jumped in earlier today...okay, it'd been heavy.

And frankly, the man was handsome too. Sharp blue eyes that reflected the dancing flames when he worked a fire. A bristle beard, trimmed in such a way he had a rugged, perpetual five-o'clock shadow. That wild, sandy-blond hair needed a trim. It fell all wrong but also...just right.

But she couldn't be with Booth if she didn't really know him. The man was buttoned up tight. Keeping secrets, she was sure of it.

Besides, letting her personal feelings get in the way had never helped her achieve her goals before. Once upon a time she'd thought she'd wanted the ring, the wedding, and the happy ending. And look how that'd turned out.

Thank You, God, for letting me see the truth about Cliff's addiction before it went too far.

Why would she let romance get in the way now, when she had her sights set on being crew chief? She needed to focus.

"Hey, Booth," Finn called. "How about another campfire story? Got anything good?"

Booth grinned. "Really? I figured you'd be sick of those stories."

"Well, since our lounge burned up today, it's not like we can watch TV," Vince said.

Logan laughed. "Yeah, man, we're a captive audience. Let's hear it."

"What about you?" He turned to look at Nova. "You up for a Crazy Henry story?"

She threw out her hands. "I'm all ears." As if he could top their real-life arsonist and would-be assassin.

"Okay, here's a story. The team was down in Middle of Nowhere, Arkansas. Intel pointed to some local hillbillies selling seed technology to foreign agents. It's middle of summer. Hotter'n the hinges on the gates of Hades—as the locals kept sayin'."

"My grandfather always said 'hotter'n the devil's armpit,'" Finn added.

"Let the man tell his story," JoJo said, tossing a napkin at Finn.

"Okay, so...Crazy Henry was captured by these zealous militia guys. They dragged him into a barn and tied him to a post. Said they were holding him until the leader came. But they made a mistake. They left him alone.

"It didn't take long before Henry got himself free. When he realized the barn was storage for bomb-making supplies, he helped himself to a little fertilizer and some chemicals. Made his own incendiary device. Ended up blowing half the barn apart. And that's how Henry rescued himself from the backwoods of Arkansas."

Nova felt her eyebrows shoot up. "Seed technology, fertilizer bomb? Really? We're supposed to believe this?"

Booth shrugged. "You'd be surprised what's happening right in your neighbor's backyard."

Like today.

A killer in her own backyard.

The gravity of Booth's statement hung heavy in the air, and one by one, the crew said good night.

"Something I said?" Booth asked.

She stood. "You sure know how to clear the room. Thanks for the story." Nova smiled to herself and headed across the field. She paused and turned around. "And…thanks for the help."

Before he could respond, Nova jogged toward the house.

"Good night, Wildfire Girl," Booth called.

Still smiling, she went inside Sophie's. The pretty rancher had offered to let "the girls" stay in her spare bedrooms, but Nova and JoJo had opted to sleep in their tents like the rest of the crew. Nova would take her up on the hot shower part though, because she hadn't worked up the nerve to go near the horses.

Inside, the shower whooshed from behind the closed bathroom door. Two doors down, Aria sat on the bed in the guest room, combing her wet hair. They'd beaten her to it, but Nova was used to cold showers. Sometimes no shower if she was working the line.

"JoJo just got in there." Aria patted the bed. "Sit. She won't be long."

Nova glanced at her pants and caught a whiff of the campfire on herself. "I'd better take the floor until I bathe."

Aria pulled a wide-tooth comb through her long blonde hair. "What's up?"

"Nothing. Tired is all." Nova sat on the floor and started to lean against the wall, then thought better of it. She'd probably leave a smear of ash and sweat on Sophie's beautiful paint.

"Out with it. You know I'm a great listener."

Nova rested her elbows on her knees. Should she open up about what was really on her mind? It was no secret that an arsonist was responsible for the fire at HQ, but few knew that Tank had been hired to kill Booth. "I've been thinking about Booth. I can't quite figure him out."

Aria lifted a brow. "Getting under your skin?"

"Yes!" She pointed. "Exactly. There's just this… this mystery behind him. He came here pretty much out of nowhere with the skills of a veteran smokejumper. And he's such a great storyteller, it makes me wonder what secrets he might be hiding in his past."

"You want to unravel the mystery?"

"Yes!" Nova furrowed her brow. "Is that so crazy?"

"Not at all." Aria paused her combing and smiled. "Look, every year we have rookies strolling in here, cocky as you please, thinking they're tougher than 'the girls'"—she made air quotes around the last part—"and you just roll with it."

"'Cause I know most of them will wash out."

"Right. But Booth is the least cocky man I've ever met, and he's the one who ruffles your feathers the most."

"That's because he's always questioning my leadership," Nova said. "Always inserting himself into what I'm doing. Like he has to protect me." Nova picked at the carpet, remembering last week. "We were out at Wildlands Academy, trying to save those teenagers from the firestorm. We were in a hurry to get the canoes in the water so we could take shelter under them. I was pulling one to the water, and Booth just took it from me and ran to the lake. I didn't ask him for help. He just took over."

Aria nodded. "Sounds like he was trying to help. You don't have to do everything alone, you know. You can ask for help."

"But I didn't need help." Her voice went up an octave. "I mean, when I need help, I'll ask for it."

Aria's hands stopped and she tilted her head. "Yeah. Sure you will. So, besides getting in your way, does he pull his weight out there?" Aria pointed her comb at the window.

Nova thought about today. The way he'd started punching line without being told. Same with the last fire. He never ran ahead of the team. Not the way she did. "He pulls more than his share."

"So why is it every time you're around him, you bristle?"

Nova picked at the laces of her boot. "Honestly?" She glanced at Aria, then back to her feet. "I don't know. It's like...I can't really get to know him. The rest of the crew—they are who they are. But Booth... there's something else there."

"Something you find...attractive?" Her friend smiled.

Nova tried to suppress a smile but failed. "Okay, maybe a little. I mean, have you looked at the guy?" She pictured him as he'd been earlier, leaning against the garage, singing to her. The crow's-feet crowding his eyes when he smiled. She shook her head. "The thing is, this job is dangerous enough on its own. I can't be distracted with romance."

Aria scooted off the bed and sat on the floor beside Nova. "You're my best friend, and you know I love you, girl, but sometimes I wonder if you have some sort of death wish like you'd rather die alone."

Nova straightened and studied her friend. "You'd rather I take someone with me? Or destroy someone's life because I'm gone?" She'd lost her parents, and it'd torn her apart. "I know how it feels to be that person left behind, and I refuse to do it to anyone else."

"What you do is dangerous, but it doesn't mean you can't fall in love and live a full life outside of this. You can have a husband. A family."

"So when the worst does happen, I leave nothing but grief in my wake? No thanks. It's better not to leave behind people who care."

Aria nudged the side of her boot. "Hey, I care!"

Nova laughed. "You know what I meant. I'd think you of all people would understand the most."

"It's normal to not want to let yourself get hurt. No one can fault you for that. But I, for one, wouldn't give up a single moment—a single memory—of my parents just to spare myself the pain of losing them." Aria wiped a tear from the corner of her eye. "I love you, and you have a whole crew that loves you—in their own way. No one will ever forget you, Nova Burns."

The image of her dad lifting her onto a horse burst into Nova's mind. She shook it away.

"That's where you're wrong." Nova stared at her friend. "I would give up every single day with them to not have to feel like this. I'd rather not have had them at all if it means it hurts this much." Get rid of it all. Amputate the whole thing. Numbness would be better than this much raw pain.

"The truth is, there will be suffering." Aria patted

Nova's hand. "Love, no matter how difficult, is worth the pain it might bring. You'll see that one day."

"Thanks. I'll think about that." Nova stood and kissed Aria on the head. "Now, I'm off to bed. Get some rest."

"Wait, what about your shower?"

"First thing tomorrow." Nova smiled and headed outside.

She lay in her tent, hands laced behind her head, staring at the stars through the skylight. No matter how long she thought about it, she couldn't figure out why she liked hearing Booth call her Wildfire Girl.

As she drifted off to sleep, the last thing she saw was Booth's smile and his eyes dancing in the firelight.

And she sorta hated herself for it.

FIVE

TODAY WAS A NEW DAY, BUT BOOTH STILL HAD OLD business to finish.

"C'mon, Crispin, answer!" Booth hung up the phone at the robotic voice that said the caller was unavailable.

Unavailable, but hopefully not dead. Crispin needed to know about the arsonist since he could probably find the guy before the sheriff did.

It all had to be connected.

Which was why, probably, he'd tossed the night away on the hard ground. Sleeping in a tent never got any easier, but somehow last night had been worse than normal. Maybe it was sleeping on the lumpy ground with a rock digging into his back. Maybe it was thoughts of Nova.

Mixed, of course, with seeing her in the fight and how Tank had hit her.

So yeah, he needed coffee in a serious way. As he came out of the barn, he headed for the campfire, where his bleary-eyed crew gathered around the dregs of the fire and sipped fresh coal-brewed coffee.

Sophie handed him a cup. "Morning. Sorry about

the sleeping accommodations." Her eyes flicked to Booth's hand kneading the stubborn knot in his shoulder.

He dropped his hand and waved off her concern. "Naw, jumpers are used to roughing it. Grateful for your hospitality though."

"Things should improve. A pal of mine has an RV lot. He's bringing a few trailers to set up. Should have kitchens and running water by day's end."

Booth nearly choked midswallow. A shower would be nice right about now. Even in a cramped RV stall. "Wait, you managed full trailers? Out here?"

She shrugged. "He owed me a favor. Figure it's the least we can do, getting you heroes settled proper."

Hero? Booth hadn't felt like a hero since he left Homeland. But nice to hear some people still considered what he did brave. "Still, that's crazy generous. Opening up your place to us and now this. Do you need any help getting spaces prepped today?"

Despite the symphony of bruises he'd earned battling the arsonist, he was still up for light duty, lending his muscle whenever possible. Might keep his thoughts from drifting toward Nova again too.

"No, no." She waved a hand. "Besides, it's your day off. Relax. Rest your bones before the next fire call comes."

Sophie was right. As much as his battered body craved collapsing into a deep sleep, wildfires waited for no man. Or woman, he amended, catching sight of Nova rolling her sleeping bag into a tight tube to keep the creepy-crawlies out.

"And that's my cue to leave," said JoJo, nodding to the sheriff cruiser pulling up the drive. "Just kidding. I planned to head into Ember to see my family. I want to hug my mom, maybe eat a homemade meal."

"I could use a burger at the Hotline," said Logan. "Maybe shoot some pool. Anyone want a ride?"

"Me," Booth said.

"Hold up, I need to have a word." Sheriff Hutchinson crooked a finger at Booth.

Booth turned to Logan. "Go on ahead. I'll catch a ride later."

With a thumbs-up, Logan and the rest headed out. Sophie disappeared into her house.

Booth followed Sheriff Hutchinson and stopped behind the patrol car. "What can I do for you, Sheriff?" Though, he had some guesses. "Any news on the arsonist?"

"My boys lifted some prints and we got a match." Hutchinson pulled out a small notebook and flipped the page. "Clyde Walsh. He'd been cooling his heels in Lompoc Federal Correctional for the last fifteen months. Got out a month ago."

"Sounds like just enough time to collect payment and start a fire." Booth clenched then unclenched his fists.

"Well, he won't be getting paid." Hutchinson scratched the side of his cheek. "He's dead."

Booth blinked. "Dead? As in murdered?"

The sheriff nodded. "Deputies found him stabbed to death in a seedy motel in the next town over."

Apparently, someone hadn't liked Clyde's work and had decided not to pay. "Any leads on who hired him?"

Hutchinson's duty belt creaked as he shifted his weight. "Still digging. Walsh is known as someone willing to get his hands dirty, and he's got a long rap sheet to prove it. Arson, assault, witness intimidation. My guess is it's the same guys who've hired him before."

Booth's jaw tightened. If only the sheriff knew the kinds of people he was likely dealing with. Dangerous people with money and connections.

He happened to glance at the barn to see Nova struggling to carry an ammo can of water. Why did she insist on pushing him away and doing everything alone? Maybe after the sheriff left, Booth would insist harder.

He turned his attention back to the sheriff. "Who's hired Walsh before?"

"Never had enough evidence to convict, but rumor had it that it was an anti-government group known as The Brothers." Hutch crossed his arms. "They're Russian sympathizers and under FBI and Homeland investigation for their dealings with the Bratva. That's the Russian mafia."

Booth's pulse kicked up. He knew where this was going, and it was nowhere good.

Hutchinson continued, "These two brothers, the Blackwell brothers, have been vocal against federal overreach. Their daddy lost the family ranch in a dispute with the Bureau of Land Management. I guess the older one, Floyd, never forgave the Feds for that. After high school he got pretty radical, talking about revolution this, Russian allies that."

Hutchinson leaned back against his cruiser. "Floyd did a couple years for selling explosives to an undercover agent...got out maybe ten years back? He dropped off the radar after that. Then his brother, Earl, shows up local a few months ago talking a big game. I figured Floyd was up to his old tricks somewhere and Earl was the bag man. Probably why he was at the camp that day."

Booth swallowed, thoughts churning. "When he died in the fire out at the Wildlands Academy," he finished.

Yeah, he definitely remembered Floyd Blackwell from his days in Homeland Security. They'd compiled a thick dossier on him and his anti-government activities. Placed him on the federal watch list.

"You think Floyd hired Walsh to torch jump base to get back at us for Earl's death?"

"Could be." The sheriff pinched his lips. "We'll keep pulling on loose ends. Meantime, you and your crew watch your backs. Call me if you catch wind of anything else strange."

Booth nodded as Hutchinson climbed into his cruiser and pulled off, the cruiser disappearing down the drive in a plume of dust.

He sighed, spine rigid with frustration. Every minute delayed gave criminals time to cover their tracks and get away while Crispin's fate hung unknown.

Glancing toward the plane, he spotted Nova lugging more supply crates. He'd planned to offer his help, but quite frankly, he wasn't sure his heart could handle the inevitable rejection right now.

Still, he couldn't ignore the protectiveness that welled up inside him when he looked at her.

With no idea of Crispin's location, and without any leads, all Booth could do was hope his friend turned up soon, preferably before whoever was after him. Sticking close to the ranch in case Crispin came looking seemed the smart play.

Physical exertion might relieve the tempest whirling, and since Nova didn't need help, he'd ask Sophie. He found her in her kitchen, cutting apples.

She smiled when she saw him. "Hey, I thought you'd gone to town with the rest."

"Decided to hang around here awhile."

"Fresh coffee if you're interested." She nodded to the pot on the counter.

"Thanks." He poured a fresh cup and took a long, appreciative sip. "Mind if I help with the horses?"

Sophie's hand went to her hip. "Why would you want to do that?"

"I dunno. Something about being around them relaxes me." Besides, mindless labor should give him time to get his thoughts in line.

"I know exactly what you mean." She grinned and tossed an apple core in the trash can. "I was just about to feed and water them, but if you can handle that, I'll get breakfast out of the oven."

"You already made breakfast? What time did you get up, woman?"

"Early. Same as always. You remember what to do?"

Booth had helped Houston take care of the horses while Sophie had been away for a weekend retreat. "A scoop of grain. Two squares of hay."

"Perfect." She squinted and held up her index finger. "Annnd...I think I've got some leftover apple crisp. I'll set it aside for when you're done."

"Oh, you rock. My favorite." Booth tossed back the remains of his coffee and handed the cup to Sophie. "Better get to it."

He crossed the pasture and headed for the weathered

barn. Already the sun was beating down through high clouds. Reports of lightning in the mountains promised more fires and another brutal shift. At least the horses would offer some measure of balm for his psyche.

Sure enough, the familiar earthy aromas of hay and grain managed to clear his head the moment he walked in.

Equine noses appeared over stall doors. "Morning, folks. Who's ready for some breakfast?" He paused and rubbed the forehead of a black mare. She nuzzled velvety lips against his palms. "Okay, okay. I got it. Food first. Affection later. Simple priorities. I get it. Eat. Move. Sleep. Repeat. Not so different than my life...minus all the complications."

Smiling to himself, he turned to get the feed and caught sight of Nova's windswept copper hair blowing in the breeze.

There was something different about her. A softness.

Arms folded, she stood in a beam of sunshine outside the threshold of the barn and wore a wide grin. "You always talk to animals?"

Booth traced the outline of his open mouth with his thumb and index finger. "Uh, yeah. It's another surprise talent of mine."

"Go figure. How'd you learn so much about horses?"

"Summer jobs." He shrugged, wanting to delve into her past rather than his. "You gonna stand out there watching or pitch in and—"

A huge white horse kicked his gate, demanding his food. Nova startled, bumping the door latch hard enough to bang the interior siding. Booth dropped the feed scoop, and Nova jumped about six inches off the ground.

"Whoops, sorry," he said. "Didn't mean to add to your already tattered nerves."

"I'm a little..." Nova pressed her palm on her chest. "A little nervous around horses, is all."

"Oh. Well...c'mon in. They're hungry, but they won't bite."

Nova shook her head.

He lifted a shoulder. "I could use the help."

A subtle grin broke through. Still, she hesitated and stayed beyond the patched door, eyes locked on the white horse.

He walked over and took her hand. "You might be scared but—"

"I'm not scared." She pulled her hand from his gasp. "It's not...that."

"Okay, how about this? You stay there, and I'll take care of feeding. At least this way, people won't make fun of me for talking to the animals." He grinned.

"Yes. I'll stay here." She pointed to the ground.

"So, uh, what's got you all spooked of these guys anyhow?"

Nova reached down and picked up a piece of hay. Wrapped it around her index finger.

"We were homesteaders, living in the mountains. My parents, they were everything. They created this haven for us. Dad was strong but also an artist. A true romantic. He didn't just bring us flowers. He'd spend hours in his pottery shed creating the perfect vase, then fill it with wildflowers and present it to my mom." Her eyes flashed bright with the memory.

"Mom, tough but tender. I swear that woman

could do anything." Nova gave a tiny shake of her head. "She taught me everything from the alphabet to what plants were safe and which were poisonous.

"When I was eight, a wildfire had been burning for days. The hotshots thought they had it under control. It blew up. Surrounded us. We were trapped."

She paused. Bright red grooves appeared on her finger where she'd wound the hay tight before unraveling it.

He quenched the crazy urge to reach out to her.

"The animals were going crazy, the horses kicking and bucking, wanting out of their stalls. Dad put me on his horse, told me to hang on tight and not to stop until I crossed the river. He slapped her hindquarters, and we took off. That was the last time I saw my parents."

"That must have been..." Booth struggled to find the right words.

"Terrifying," she finished. "I rode that horse until exhaustion, but I made it across the river." She let the hay fall to the ground. "I never saw them again."

He swallowed hard. After that, he wasn't sure how she could face raging wildfires but not the animals that'd saved her life. Trauma did strange things to people, and it wasn't for Booth to judge how Nova carried hers with her every day. But matching what she'd gone through with the Nova he'd seen walking through fire to save lives made perfect sense.

"Know what's the worst part?" She drew an arc in the dirt with the toe of her boot.

There was a worse part?

"My mom was nine months pregnant." Her voice dipped low. "I've always wondered why he put me on that horse instead of her. He could've saved two lives..."

Booth knew a little something about the guilt Nova carried—the depth of loss, second-guessing a decision you made in a split second. It was enough to drive a person mad. "Your dad faced an impossible situation, and in that moment, he made a choice—an agonizing one. Sometimes, life throws us into situations where there are no good answers. I don't think it means you have to close yourself off."

"Funny you're the one saying that." She folded her arms. "Care to share something from your past?"

He stared at all the raw pain in her expression, knowing exactly what that felt like. Two words ran through his mind.

National security.

"That's what I thought." Nova turned and walked out of the barn.

Booth watched her leave.

Not only could he not tell her who he really was.

He also couldn't tell her why his past had to stay a secret.

Nova rushed from the barn before Booth could stop her.

Aria had told her to open herself up to what could be. As if that ever did anyone any good. This was just more proof that Booth wasn't going to change her life—as much as she might want that to be true.

Last night, and again just now, her walls had cracked. Against her better judgment, she'd let Booth inside. Exposed her underbelly. Shown weakness.

And she already sensed how bad that could turn out.

The truth was, fire didn't frighten Nova anymore. The real threat, the vulnerability she fiercely guarded against, was the possibility of losing someone she loved in the flames.

Memories of her parents had left her with a painful throbbing deep in her soul. All she wanted to do was drop to her knees in a patch of scrub grass and suck deep lungfuls of clear mountain air until the pain retreated back to its dull ache.

Peace. She had to find peace.

But that required falling apart, confronting the pain and scars of her past. And she couldn't bring herself to do it. Not yet.

Stalks of dry grass crackled under her boots as she straightened. Get it together, Burns. Feeling sorry for herself wouldn't solve her problems.

Jude County's fire rescue trailer sat in front of Sophie's house. Good.

The command center would remind her of priorities—the family legacy she aimed to honor by making crew chief someday. It was the one relationship in which she'd risk everything, and right now she could get some work done to that end. Make sure Miles knew she was on the ball.

Tucker's absence was her opportunity to step things up. Prove herself.

The trailer door stood open, but she rapped her knuckles against the frame anyway. "Knock knock?"

Miles Dafoe, the county's fire commander, glanced up from a detailed topo map spread across the table. He had his shirt sleeves folded up and reading glasses perched on his nose. His dark hair had more salt than pepper in it these days. "Come on in."

She stepped inside, zeroing in on the Incident Status whiteboard listing resources in staging. "Looks like we're still sitting on four helicopters, three hotshot crews..."

"Yep, plus the three smokejumper loads already out." He tapped a Sharpie against pursed lips. "I was afraid we might need more air attack when that lightning blew through yesterday, but seems they've got the range fires pretty well contained."

"For now." She scanned scattered pins stuck in the map, denoting fire locations. "If this wind keeps up, though..."

"We're watching those storms, same as you. General briefings at 0700, 1300 and 1900 hours if you want the full weather and operations update."

She nodded. "Copy that."

Nova respected Miles. Some of the guys joked he was a little OCD about protocol and paperwork, but after twenty years working wildfires, Miles had a good reason for sweating the details.

Protocols saved lives.

Miles folded his arms. "How are Tucker's crews handling things?"

And there it was. The question that had needled since the accident that'd taken out their crew chief. Oh sure, Miles was sly about it, not coming right out and asking who he should tap for acting crew chief. But they both knew what he meant.

Her pulse kicked as she considered responses. Play it humble? Ultraconfident?

The line between capable and conceited was thin.

"Honestly?" She tempered her tone even as

ambition burned hot. "The team needs a leader. I've stepped up. Tried to take the lead. But without someone in charge, we're not the cohesive unit Tucker built."

"Tucker runs a tight crew. Hate to see him laid up, but he knew something could go wrong out there at any moment. He's trained you to be smokejumpers he can count on."

Okay, so no glowing nominations yet. She tried another angle, hoping her readiness showed. "I'm happy to take on more responsibility wherever it helps most."

"With this wind, it's gonna be a chess match balancing containment with safety. Good leadership is key in the field." His hand went to his chin, scrutinizing her through narrowed eyes. "Here's the deal. I wanted to check the landscape before restructuring leadership. Tucker runs a top-notch crew deployment model. Hate tampering when it's not broke."

He raised his palms. "But maybe this unfortunate accident is the nudge we need to shake things up. Give capable prospects like yourself a chance to step up."

A smile teased the corner of her mouth at hearing exactly what she'd wanted. "Appreciate the vote of confidence."

"For now, I'll let the crew keep rolling as is." His mouth slanted. "Of course, that could change should we find the right person. You know your fires. Far more than most. But you also need to know how to manage and work with your team. How to trust them. Do that, and I'll see if you can take Tucker's place."

"Yes, sir." Nova turned to leave but halted midstep.

There, outside the corral, stood Booth. In the shade of the barn, his forearms rested atop the weathered rails. Laugh lines etched deeper as he watched the antics of the horses jostling in the field. He had a day's scruff and tousled, windblown hair. How someone could appear both soft and rugged at the same time baffled her.

He shifted sideways and caught sight of her. Lifted his chin and looked away.

She couldn't deny being attracted. But it wasn't only his physical appeal needling her determination. What really shook her was how he kept surprising her. Like listening to her story in the barn.

And frustrating her by telling none of his own.

But she'd been a little sensitive earlier, and blast if she didn't need to apologize for it.

Nova squared her shoulders and cut across the field, straight toward Booth. "Look, I'm sorry for walking away like that. It's just..." She sighed. "You're such a mystery. And I opened up something deep inside by telling you my story. Sure, most everyone knows my parents died, but they don't know how deep the wound goes. I didn't want you to see that side of me. That...weakness."

There was a full twenty seconds of silence. Nova swallowed and prepared to walk off when Booth finally spoke.

"You see that mare?" He pointed to the brown horse Nova had fed earlier. "The white guy keeps nipping but she doesn't flinch."

Nova studied the old horse, noting that tiny detail. "Yeah. She's got no reaction."

"Right. Total emotional resilience. My sister was like that." He paused. "I mean…in big, emotional moments, most people panic or freeze. But Raelynn always knew what to do. Saved my hide more times than I can count."

She glanced at him. "You have a sister?"

"Three years older than me." He snagged a tendril of hair blowing across his forehead and pushed it back. "I was an ornery little punk. Constantly getting in trouble."

"Now, that I believe." Nova smiled.

"Anyway…" He shifted sideways, one elbow resting on his bent knee so he faced her. His golden tone turned solemn.

The humor in her dissipated.

"When Raelynn was twelve, she wanted to be first across the lake soon as it froze. I warned her to wait till Dad checked it to be sure the ice was thick, but she laughed, calling me a sissy." Booth studied his palm, tracing lines only he could see.

In her mind, Nova could see a little girl with Booth's eyes, teasing her brother.

"I finally got up nerve to cross, but about fifteen yards from shore, I crashed through." He flexed his hand open and closed. "I'll never forget the sound. Sharp cracks like thunderclaps, and I plunged into that dark water. It happened so fast I didn't have time to breathe."

Nova's chest constricted. She could almost smell the cold. Hear the sound of water rushing in her ears. That helpless animal panic—the same panic she'd felt on that horse, fighting for her life.

"I managed to crawl back up, but I couldn't lift myself out. Raelynn army-crawled out and was trying to pull me up when the whole sheet gave way." He squeezed his eyes shut as if to block the images. "She had me almost out when it collapsed, taking her under. I used the broken shelf to get up, but she was too far down. By the time Dad got there, she..." His jaw hardened. "She'd been under too long."

Nova watched muscles pulse along his stubbled jaw. Her own chest squeezed, recognizing the bottomless guilt and crushing helplessness.

Before she could stop herself, she covered his fist with her palm. "You were just a kid, Booth. It couldn't be your fault."

"Maybe if I'd waited for Dad...or run faster to get help"—his shoulder jerked—"I could have saved her instead of myself."

"Did your dad blame you?"

"I don't know. We haven't spoken in five years, but not because of that. It's the job, you know?"

Nova did know. It was easy to get wrapped up in fire season. The crew became your family. "What about your mom?"

"Mom works long hours as an attorney, and I have a younger brother in law school. They spend a lot of time together. Have more in common. Last time I spoke to my father we had an argument. He said I should just get over what happened to Raelynn." Booth paused and Nova gave him time to finish. "I guess I don't know how to forget what happened and stop second-guessing that day."

Her next breath clogged hard in her chest. She gave his hand a fierce squeeze. "I know what it's like to live with saving yourself while someone else dies. People think time heals the hurt, but all it does is turn it into a specter, and we have to live with that. It haunts us the rest of our lives."

Blue eyes flashed understanding. "Yeah." His whisper softened. "Yeah, it does."

Their hands remained stacked. In a lot of ways, they were the same.

Nova hadn't realized that, but it made sense now. They both hesitated to let people below the surface. To where the sorrow lived.

Nova swiped her thumb over his knuckles, wishing she could erase the old scars. Wishing she were bold enough to climb inside his vault of pain and help him heal.

She cleared the gravel from her throat. "Guilt eats us alive, even when there's nothing we could have done differently."

Booth turned his palm up to cradle hers. Calluses aligning in a broken mosaic. "No matter how far I go, I can't seem to outrun my past mistakes."

Nova nodded. Since the fire that had taken her family, she'd only operated in survival mode, caging her deepest longings, protecting her heart behind fortified walls.

But at that moment, sitting with Booth, the walls looked more like a self-imposed prison.

Booth's thumb stroked tiny circles that sent a vibration up her arm.

A nicker snapped her gaze left. The brown mare bucked. Kicked her back feet and bucked again. The horse galloped toward them.

Nova's breath seized.

Then she was falling backward.

Nova crashed against the sun-warmed cotton

covering Booth's chest. Muscled arms wrapped around her waist, bringing their faces inches apart.

Electricity arced in the airless space between them.

Towering over her, his soft blue eyes searched her face. "You okay?" A smile teased the edges of his mouth.

"Uh-huh." Pulse tapping, Nova's gaze drifted to his mouth, hovering close. Did he kiss as good as he smelled?

Whoa.

She blinked hard.

What was she thinking? Twenty-four hours ago, the man was driving her crazy.

Now, maybe a different kind of crazy.

He pulled her a fraction closer. Lips a breath apart. "You…sure?"

"Hey, Booth! You've got—" Sophie stopped dead in her tracks and stared at them. "Oh, um. Sorry." Flustered, she turned and bolted into the barn.

Great. Booth had been about to kiss her, and blast if she hadn't been about to let him.

SIX

ALL AT ONCE, NOVA STIFFENED IN HIS ARMS. HE loosened his grip, and she extracted herself from his embrace. Made a beeline for the house, mumbling something about macaroni and cheese.

A gust of wind blew stray locks that she swiped as if swatting insects. She stumbled on a rock, caught herself and muttered again.

Booth pressed his lips tight. He didn't want to laugh, but he sure was getting a kick out of her fluster.

He was in so much trouble here.

Oh, how badly he wanted a chance. Wanted her. Not just the kiss he was sure they'd been about to have, but waking up beside her smile. Exploring life's adventures together. Building something lasting from the ashes they'd risen from.

Regret rose under his ribs. The weight of his own past pressed down. That life was nothing but a dream when you had enemies trained to use loved ones as leverage.

Whatever burned between them, he had to let it

simmer. Keep things professional. For both their sakes.

The horses whinnied and trotted to one corner of the corral. He followed their gazes to see Sophie standing there.

Booth straightened from the rail he'd slumped against. "You were coming to tell me something?"

Sophie smiled and paused to pet the muzzles tracking her along the fence. "I just wanted to let you know a package came for you. I left it on the porch."

"Package? That's some forwarding service. I just got here."

"Maybe one of the guys brought it from jump base?" She turned her palms up and shrugged.

"Thanks, and if you need any help with the apple crisp leftovers"—he patted his stomach—"I'm your man."

"You'll have to fight Houston for it!" she called over her shoulder.

Booth jogged to the porch and found a small box with his name written in block letters. No return address. Inside was an ancient looking phone wrapped in a plastic grocery sack. He turned it on. A red icon on the Messages app indicated one new text.

Must talk. Meet at film set jail. Respond with C to confirm.

Booth stared at the phone.

Respond with C? Was this Crispin's desperate attempt to meet away from Sophie and the rest of the smokejumper crew? Or was it someone else altogether?

After a few seconds of mental gymnastics, he

slipped the phone into his back pocket. He needed to figure out what was going on before he responded. If it was Crispin, this could be a chance for Booth to get his life back.

He saw Houston opening the door to his truck and jogged over. "Hey, you heading into town?"

Houston paused. "Yeah. Need a ride?"

"If you don't mind. I'm meeting a friend near the movie set. That too far out of your way?"

"Nah, it's on the way. Hop in."

"Just a sec." Booth jogged over to where JoJo was oiling the chain saws before packing them in fire boxes.

"JoJo, I'm running into town with Houston. I should be back before my shift starts."

JoJo scrunched her face. "Okay, but why are you telling me?"

"Cell coverage is spotty up there. I was going to tell Nova in case a call came in, but..." He trailed off, not wanting to tell JoJo how their near kiss had sent Nova scurrying to get away.

JoJo's eyebrows arched.

"Never mind. I'll text her."

JoJo shrugged. "Good idea since I guess she's sorta in charge for now."

Of course Nova would step up like that with Tucker out. That was her style. "Well, if she asks you..." Booth didn't finish. He turned and pulled the burner phone from his front pocket.

He typed one letter and hit Send.

With his own phone, he sent a text to Nova updating her on where he'd be for the next few hours. His thumb hovered over the smile emoji. Better not press his luck.

A few minutes later, Booth was rumbling down the road in Houston's green-and-tan behemoth from the nineties. Cool wind rushed through their open windows. Booth rested his elbow outside and watched the sun streaking through the boughs of towering pines. A cloud of brown dust swirled behind them and never seemed to settle.

Houston mirrored Booth, elbow propped on the windowsill, hand draped over the steering wheel. "I thought the movie was all wrapped and that old town was deserted again."

"Thought I'd go take a look now that all the fuss has died down and security isn't so tight." Booth didn't want to answer a lot of questions and decided to change the subject. "Man…without Tucker, our crew feels like a ship without a rudder."

"We run pretty smooth on our own. Besides, Nova's stepped up to the helm."

"Only because she's so headstrong. Logan has more experience leading. I don't know why he's letting her overshadow him. I thought he wanted to be crew chief."

Houston flattened his lips, thinking. "Pushing himself into the slot won't make it happen."

"Someone should tell Nova that. She's pushing herself too hard. Some of the risks she takes…" He shook his head. "She's gonna get herself killed."

"And you think it's your job to keep that from happening?"

Booth already had a job. Two if he counted smokejumping. "I can't always be there to protect her. I know that."

"You see those trees?" Houston pointed.

Booth watched the trees passing by, their trunks blackened by the recent wildfire. "Yeah?"

"On the outside, all you see is charred bark. They've been through the fire, and they look dead. But take a pocketknife and peel back that burnt outer bark. There's life underneath. Now, we could run around stripping every tree, revealing the raw heartwood, but that would expose it to the elements too soon. The first frost, the next fire—either would kill it. The tree needs that protective layer a while longer."

The blaze that'd killed Nova's family had reshaped her the same way wildfires reshaped the landscape. "Are you saying Nova was burned and she needs more time to heal?"

Houston laughed. "No, brother. I'm saying we're all like those trees."

"I get that. But what if she's killed before she ever finds healing?"

"What if *you* are?" Houston shot him a look. "We all come out here to find something. If Nova's named crew chief, God already knew it. If I'm killed in the next fire, it's no surprise to Him. We get our true identity from God, not our jobs. It's why we've got to make the most of the time we have."

Easy for Houston to say. God had taken Booth's identity away and left him stranded in Jude County living a lie. "I don't know. Lately I've been feeling like I've lost everything that defined me. Some days I don't know who I am."

"I know how you feel." Houston shifted in his seat. "When I got fired from my job as a youth pastor in Last Chance County, I lost who I was. I'd put my job on a pedestal and made it my everything. But God showed me that's not what He wanted from me. Now my identity is wrapped up in God, not my job."

But maybe Houston was right. Maybe there was something more God was doing here, and Booth had to open his eyes to see it.

They rode in silence but for the rattle of the pickup bouncing over the rutted road. Houston came to an intersection and slowed to a stop.

"This is good," Booth said. "Drop me here."

Houston's brow furrowed. "You sure? It's probably another mile down that road."

Booth hopped out and slammed the door. He leaned through the open window. He had no idea what he was walking into, and he wasn't about to drag Houston into danger. "Nah, it'll be a breeze without my pack-out." Honestly, packing out over a hundred pounds of tools and gear was the hardest part of his job.

"Shoot me a text if you need a lift back."

Booth patted the roof. "Will do. Thanks for the lift. And for the chat. It helped."

Houston waved and turned the corner, heading toward Ember.

Booth waited until the truck topped the hill and disappeared before he took off down the road to the abandoned Western town that had been rebuilt and redressed for the movie this summer.

The walk was good. Fresh air. Summer sun. Jagged tops of the Kootenai mountains as the perfect backdrop for the little town.

He kicked a rock and sent it skittering across the wooden sidewalk.

Booth heard a noise. He stopped midstep and listened.

Grunting. A hard knock. The sound of a fist hitting flesh. A moan.

He raced down the sidewalk. His boots thudded a steady beat on the worn wooden planks. The jail's small window allowed Booth to peek inside.

A battered Crispin came into focus. He'd been tied to a metal chair. Bound by his hands and feet. Beaten, his face swollen and purple.

"Where is it!" A man with greasy brown hair wore tattered jeans and a threadbare shirt. He stood about six feet away with a gun pointed at Booth's former partner.

This wasn't Walsh the arsonist, and it wasn't Floyd. It was someone Booth didn't recognize.

"I'm not afraid to end this right here!" The way the man's hand vibrated as he thrust the gun out toward Crispin said otherwise.

Crispin flicked his gaze to Booth, eyes flashing with anger.

Booth's muscles coiled.

Decision time.

He crouched and duckwalked toward the doorway. Pressed his back to the wall. No time for second-guessing. He had to save Crispin.

Booth burst into the room. Ran flat-out and sacked the gunman from behind.

A grunt erupted as, together, they slammed into the floor in a tangled mess of limbs. Booth roared and wrestled the attacker, trying to pin him down. The gun went flying. It clattered across the wood planks and slipped between the bars of the jail. The attacker scrambled for it, but Booth grabbed his ankle and dragged him backward.

The gunman rolled over and smashed his other

boot into Booth's stomach. A low growl escaped Booth's throat.

From his chair, Crispin strained against his bindings, rocking his chair back. Booth tossed the small pocketknife he always carried into Crispin's lap. He put himself between the gunman and Crispin.

The attacker backed up. "Who are you?"

That was the question Booth had been wrestling with for months. But not the response this guy was looking for. "I'm the guy who's taking you to jail."

The man sneered. "I don't think so." He charged Booth.

Booth caught him by the shoulders and spun him into the wall. The attacker cried out as his nose smashed against solid wood. Blood bubbled out of his nostrils.

Crispin rocked the metal chair forward, sending it crashing into the gunman's legs. The attacker cursed and stumbled into the jail bars. He dropped and stuck his hand through the slats.

"No!" Booth ran for the man, jumping over Crispin, who'd just freed himself.

He was too slow.

The attacker grabbed the gun, rolled over, and aimed it at Crispin.

A gunshot blasted.

Nova stomped on the brakes and slammed her Bronco into Park at the abandoned one-horse ghost town slash movie set. She'd been around guns her entire life. There was no mistaking it.

That sound had been a gunshot.

She reached under her seat and pulled her Glock 21 out of the holster. With the bears that roamed the woods, she usually carried the .45 ACP hand cannon on her jumps. She'd shoved it into her car to lock it up after the last fire.

Booth hadn't been responding to her calls and texts. Of course, she hadn't responded to his at first. That moment with Booth had her rattled, and she couldn't trust herself with words. But work took precedence, and they'd been called out on an emergency deployment minutes after Booth's text saying he'd hitched a ride here.

But why? What was he doing here anyway?

It didn't matter. If someone was shooting at him, maybe it would be helpful to have someone shooting back, at least to lay down some cover for him to get away and give authorities time to get here.

A man crashed out of the movie-set jail covered in blood.

"Hey! Stop!" Nova shouted before her brain comprehended the danger.

What was she doing? The man could shoot her dead on the spot. She didn't see a gun, but that didn't mean he wasn't armed.

The man cast a quick glance over his shoulder, still running. Their eyes locked for a fleeting second before he disappeared around the corner.

Oh no...Booth!

Nova sprinted across the gravel road and slid to a stop in the doorway of the darkened jail.

Booth was on his knees, hands pressed into the shoulder of a man on the floor. "Crispin! C'mon, man. Stay with me."

She gaped at the man on the floor. "Is that…is that Sophie's brother?"

Booth looked up, eyes wide, hair falling into his face. He shook it back. "Nova? What are you doing here?"

"I—"

"Never mind. Do you have your phone? I think mine fell out in Houston's truck."

"Yeah, I tried to call you but kept getting voicemail." She crossed the room and crouched beside Booth.

Crispin looked bad. Real bad. One eye was closed, and she doubted he could open it, even if he tried. He had a split lip. Cuts and scrapes on his face. A gash along his hair line. Someone had worked him over.

Booth had taken his flannel off and wadded it up as a makeshift bandage. He held pressure on Crispin's shoulder. "It's a through and through. Don't think it hit anything vital. It's the rest of it I'm worried about."

"What can I do?"

Booth shot her a worried glance. "Call an ambulance."

Crispin groaned. "No…no hospital."

"Sorry, pal. You've been shot. Need to get you patched up and back to work." Booth flicked his eyes to Nova and mouthed, *Call.*

Nova nodded and tucked her weapon into her waistband. She shuffled to the doorway and scanned the area for signs of the gunman. He was probably long gone by now. Whoever he was.

There were so many questions running through her head, but first, she made the call and requested an air ambulance.

Once she confirmed their location, dispatch said,

"The medevac chopper will be on the ground in thirty minutes. Can you package the patient?"

"I have a medical kit. Best I can do is first aid and cover him with a blanket."

"That'll do. Keep him stationary. Let the EMTs move him." Dispatch wanted Nova to stay on the line, but her battery was low. "I'll keep my phone close. Call when they're a few minutes out."

She ran to her SUV and grabbed the supplies. Returned to Booth and knelt across from him. "Medevac will be here soon. Let me bandage his wound." She popped the latch on her kit and found the gauze pads.

Crispin opened one eye. "Where'd he go?"

"You scared him off." Booth continued to hold pressure on the wound. "But you look like you went a few rounds with Conor McGregor. What happened here?"

Crispin's eye rolled to look at her, then back to Booth.

"That's my friend Nova. She's gonna clean you up. You can speak freely with her here." Booth looked at her and arched a brow.

She nodded. He wanted to trust her with the parts he'd kept secret all this time. She wasn't about to break his trust. "We need to get his shirt off, but hold pressure until I tell you."

"I remember. Under the canoes." Crispin licked his bloodied lip. "It's Floyd. Wants revenge…Blames us for Earl's death. Hired…men. Wants…wants to find…" He trailed off.

"Don't worry about that now. Save your energy." Nova pulled gloves on and cut up the middle of Crispin's shirt and along the shoulder seam.

Booth lifted his hands long enough for Nova to peel the shirt back. The bullet wound was a small hole about the size of her index finger. Booth was right. The shot had gone through Crispin's shoulder muscle and exited. It looked clean, but doctors would need to verify with an X-ray.

She covered the front wound with a stack of gauze pads and taped it down. "Roll him so I can do the back."

Nova waited until Booth was by her side. "Roll on three. One…two…three."

Booth rolled Crispin enough for Nova to get the bandage in place.

Crispin grunted.

She taped it down fast, and they lowered Crispin. She covered him with a blanket up to his chin and handed Booth a wet wipe for the blood on his hands.

Instead of using it himself, Booth wiped Crispin's chin. "Why'd you come here, buddy?"

"I…I had to tell you…" Crispin's eye fought to stay open, lost.

"Tell me? Tell me what?" Booth looked to her.

Nova put her fingers to Crispin's neck. "Pulse is good."

Her cell phone rang. She pulled off the bloody gloves and answered. "Burns."

"We're landing in two minutes. Clear the area," Medevac said.

"Copy." She disconnected and slid her phone into her back pocket. "Medevac is incoming. I'll go meet them."

Booth nodded and continued to watch Crispin. She stood and squeezed Booth's shoulder. He placed his hand over hers. "Thanks."

Nova swallowed and went outside into the afternoon sun.

The thump-thump-thump of the helicopter's rotors grew louder on approach.

She was all kinds of twisted up inside seeing Booth so worried about Crispin. This was why she avoided relationships. Pain.

The helicopter made a sharp turn before setting down in the clearing. In a matter of seconds, the EMTs unloaded with their gear and ran to Crispin.

The small one-room jail was too crowded, so Nova waited outside with Booth. They stood in silence as the EMTs loaded Crispin onto a gurney and hurried him to the air ambulance.

Almost as quickly as it had arrived, the chopper ascended.

Booth turned and walked off.

"Wait." She trotted after him. "Where are you going?"

He kept walking. "To find whoever did this."

"We don't have time for that right now." She grabbed him by the bicep.

Booth spun around. The muscles in his jaw flinched. "We can't just let this guy get away. That's already happened once."

"I agree. But that's what the police are for." She released his arm. "They sent a plane up with a six-man crew this morning, but the fire is dangerously close to Snowhaven. We have to go. Aria has the plane ready."

Booth stared at her for an uncomfortable moment. "Look, there's something going on here that's bigger than you and me. Bigger than wildfires and arsonists. And I have to stop it."

"Is this another one of your ultrafantastical stories about rogue CIA operatives and terrorists?"

Booth turned and marched down the sidewalk.

"Wait. I'm sorry." Nova followed him. "Where are you going?"

"What's it look like? I'm going after him."

"Please...tell me the truth. What's this all about?"

Booth spun to face her. "Look, whoever is behind this set fire to jump base. Nearly killed you and a civilian. Now Crispin?" He shook his head. "I can't just walk away."

Being in this old Western town turned movie set had him talking like he was a Texas Ranger or something. There was no sense in reminding him he wasn't a cop, because she'd already done that. "Come on, we need to get back to the ranch. We've got to stop this fire before it reaches the town."

"Not this time." The planks creaked as Booth strode across the wooden sidewalk.

She quickened her pace and stepped in front of him, blocking his path. "Booth, the team needs you. I need you. You're one of the best smokejumpers—"

"I'm not a smokejumper!"

Nova blinked.

He raked a hand through his hair. Stray locks fell back into his eyes. "I'm a special agent with the Department of Homeland Security."

She stared at him for almost a full ten seconds. Then, "I think all these Crazy Henry stories have you mixing up reality with fantasy." She almost laughed, but the intensity of his gaze said he was serious.

"You don't get it." He pushed his hair back and held it with both hands, palms covering his eyes. "Ugh!"

Wait. The secrets. The closed-up conversations. "Is this the secret you've been hiding?"

He dropped his hands. Closed the distance between them. Took her hand and clasped it in his. Fixed his ocean-blue eyes on her. "I'm not who you think I am. I'm a smokejumper, but only because it's my cover. I'm in WITSEC."

"Witness protection? As a smokejumper? Isn't the whole point of the program to keep someone alive? This job isn't exactly safe."

"It is remote."

He was serious, wasn't he?

"All these attacks?" She lifted her chin in the direction of the jail. "They're because of you?" She laced her fingers through his.

"I—I think so." He looked down. "I'm still trying to work this out."

She looked at their hands clasped in one big tangle of fingers and warmth. If what he said was true, he had an impossible choice. "Look, you don't have to tell me anything. I'm sorry about all this, but that gunman is long gone, and Crispin is safe. I'm not going to tell you what to do—"

"That's a first."

"Yeah. Okay. I deserve that."

He'd finally given her a piece of his past, and while she wanted to keep digging, they had to leave this behind and get to work.

"All I know is the fire is bad, and if we don't go, the whole town could be destroyed. There're more lives at stake. The crew needs you." She reached up and brushed his hair out of his eyes. "I need you out there, just until I have reinforcements."

"Okay, yeah. You're right." He pushed out a long

breath. "I won't have anything to go on until I can get to the hospital and talk to Crispin. Besides, I want to be there for you. Always."

Nova tucked her lips together and nodded. She hadn't been asking him to make some sort of life-altering commitment to her. Just to do his job by her side.

But their talk earlier had pulled down a few of her walls, and she was starting to open her heart to this man.

Whoever he was.

SEVEN

Booth was no expert, but he'd fought enough wildfires to know if the wind kept pushing, they'd be pulling an all-nighter. He'd dropped in with Nova a few hours ago and hadn't stopped working since. Not even when the sun had sunk below the horizon and darkness had settled around them.

With each scrape of his Pulaski, he tried to connect the dots between Earl and Floyd to Crispin and the man who'd shot him. Sophie had texted to let him know that Crispin's gunshot wound didn't need surgery, and they were keeping him overnight for a concussion. At least Booth knew where to find him. Worse case, he still had the burner phone.

His team—Eric, Finn, Vince, and the rookie named Rico—pressed ahead, clearing brush and felling the most dangerous snags so a fire line could be built by the hotshot crews that followed.

Nova was out there somewhere, walking the line, checking on the other smokejumpers and barking orders as acting crew chief. She'd had questions about his witness protection, but they hadn't had time to talk with the crew around. Frankly, he owed her an explanation after she'd stumbled into not one but two assassination attempts.

He scraped flaming debris away from the bottom of a dead tree six feet thick. The massive snag burned red hot clear to the top. Trees like this were called widow makers. Better they cut it down than it fall and crush someone. Booth wouldn't let an assassin *or* a tree kill him if he could help it.

He paused and leaned on his Pulaski. "Good enough?"

"I think I can get in there." Rico tossed his Pulaski down and picked up the chain saw. Firelight shimmered off his sweaty face. "Watch that hot mama right there. If she breaks off, I'm a goner." With the tip of the chain saw blade, he pointed to a massive tree limb twenty feet overhead. It glowed hot and spat bits of burning bark at them.

Booth stood about ten feet back and acted as lookout while Rico buried the chain saw into the tree. The rookie jumper was an expert sawman from his days on the hotshot crew and had the tree down in minutes. They moved up to the next snag while Eric cranked up his saw and started bucking the log.

They made slow progress, but at least it was progress. One good thing—all this time scraping and digging had given him plenty of opportunity to berate himself for telling Nova he was in WITSEC.

She'd promised to keep it on the low down. Or was it down low? He could never remember.

He was pretty sure his cover was blown anyway, since Walsh had set fire to jump base. Then the man attacking Crispin, whoever that man had been. He'd been hired by Floyd to find something. To beat information out of Crispin.

Floyd had to know Booth and Crispin had been partners.

Which meant Floyd knew about the missing nuke and could tell the world who Booth really was.

If Crispin didn't make it, then it didn't matter who Booth had been. He'd stay here in Ember, unable to return to his job in Homeland, ever.

They were looking for someone to pin things on, and he made a great scapegoat.

"Booth, man. What're you doing?" Rico clinked his Pulaski against Booth's. "You've been breaking the same spot for a while, dude. Get your head outta the clouds."

"Shut up and get on the saw," Booth teased. "Unless it's too hot in there. Maybe your delicate rookie skin can't take the heat."

"Whatever." Rico nudged past Booth. "You just keep to your daydreaming. I'll take care of the rest."

The gall of that newb.

Nova seemed to think them doing their jobs was more important than his case. But she didn't know the risks. The wildfire might destroy one town, but in the wrong hands, a nuke could destroy an entire state.

Crispin only had one partner, and he'd made it clear he'd rather have zero. But now that Crispin was in the hospital, who was going to stop Floyd from finding the missing nuke?

If Nova knew what was at stake, she might realize his skills as a federal agent were more valuable than his skills as a smokejumper.

He shouldn't have come out here. He should've gone to work on his real job.

"Precious cargo coming through," Eric said,

coming to stand beside Booth. He lifted his chin at Rico. "Surprised you're still on your feet, Rookie."

"Someone's gotta carry the weight around here. You look like you've been lifting more donuts than dumbbells, old man." Rico brought the tree down. "And that is how it's done."

A headlamp flashed through the smoke, and Nova appeared against a backdrop of burning forest. Somehow, the fire in her eyes sparked brighter than the light of the fire. "We've got a spot fire picking up steam and heading for an abandoned mining claim, so you three are with me."

Booth refilled his water jug and hefted his PG bag. Slung his Pulaski over his shoulder and caught up to Nova. "Can you afford to pull three off the crew for a spot fire?"

"Politics. Historical preservation of the Kootenai National Forest or some such thing," she said.

"Is there anything even left out there to save?"

"Old cabins, mostly."

"Anyone live up there?"

"No, it's administered land. Hikers might stop over, but the area is so remote I doubt it."

"Hey, Nova," Rico called from behind. "You're friends with that pilot Aria, right?"

Nova scrunched up her face and flicked a questioning glance at Booth. "Um, yeah. Why?"

"I was thinkin' about asking her out. Could you put in a good word for me?"

"Sure." She smiled at Booth. "If you carry my pack out when we're done."

"Pfft. No way. Carry your own stuff."

"Rico, you dummy. That was a test," Eric said.

"Well, ain't no girl worth that. I'm already carrying the saw pack and my own junk."

"When will you learn, man?" Eric laughed. "There's always pain involved when it comes to women."

Rico snorted. "Guess I'll be single forever."

Nova shook her head. "Hopeless."

Booth laughed. "No pain, no gain."

Rico and Eric fell back a few yards, talking about the new hire at the Hotline. A blonde bombshell, to hear Rico talk about her. Booth hadn't noticed. He only had eyes for a certain bossy redhead.

The mine was a mile-long hike up a steep slope beyond the head of the fire. It had several structures scattered throughout a flat area. Booth imagined the mine had once housed multiple families, but now it was being reclaimed by nature. Two smaller cabins had collapsed in on themselves, but the main log cabin looked to be in pretty good shape. Well, other than the dilapidated porch, busted glass windows, and overgrown vegetation. Several smaller sheds and outbuildings dotted the landscape.

Nova dropped her pack and chugged about a third of her water. "Okay, guys. I think the waste rock dump will hold the left flank, but we'll need to keep the fire from running up that ridge behind the cabins. With this wind, it'll push the fire right over our heads, and we'll have a blowup on our hands."

Booth had been there, done that. Two years ago, a fifty-five-mile-an-hour wind gust had caused a fire to take off. In less than an hour, the fire had gone from six acres to a thousand, closing off his escape route. He'd been forced into his fire shelter. It'd saved his life, but the whole time he'd felt like the foil-wrapped potatoes he tossed into the campfire.

One of the few times fighting wildfires when he'd really thought he wouldn't make it out alive. He stared at the burning treetops waving in the wind. "Looks like we have our work cut out for us."

Rico and Eric began grumbling and unpacking their gear.

The head of the fire sizzled and snapped. Booth paused. "Shh! You hear that?"

Everyone stared at a section of flames roaring far above the tree line. Black smoke billowed from the spot.

Eric created a visor with his hand. "What the heck is it?"

A rumbling sound rippled from somewhere in the fire followed by a giant crash.

Booth stepped in front of Nova.

The trees cracked and swayed. A booming kathump, kathump shook the ground.

Something was coming for them.

Booth saw it. A great big fiery log the size of a rocket came bouncing down the hill, spraying embers and igniting smaller fires everywhere.

"Nova..." Booth swallowed. "I think we've got a big problem."

Nova watched as the log hurtled down the north side of the hill, hit a boulder, bounced over the waste rock dump, and landed with an earth-pounding boom in a copse of dead spruce.

A fire swooshed to life.

"Yep. Big problem," Nova said.

"Did you see that thing? Ooo-whee," Rico hooted. "Like a log rolled right out of a giant's fireplace!"

"Sure did," Eric said. "What was that thing?"

"A pylon from that old ore bin up the hill." Booth pointed.

The burning log had lit a spot fire that had already spread to the size of a volleyball court. If she didn't get her crew to contain it, Booth's "big trouble" would be the understatement of the year.

"Okay, Booth, Rico. Get on that before it gets out of hand. We need that fire banked." Nova palmed her radio and called headquarters. The reply never came.

She hadn't picked Booth, Eric, and Rico because they'd been goofing off. Quite the opposite. They were the fastest guys on the crew. Rico might be a rookie, but his years as a hotshot gave him more experience in wildland firefighting than Booth. It was why she'd put them together.

Eric was a bit more of a wildcard. Seasoned enough to do the work in half the time, but more likely to take risks. Risks, she had to admit, that he could handle most of the time.

She holstered her walkie and picked up her gear. "Let's get to work. I should have radio signal up on the ridge. I'll call in the water drop."

Rico grabbed his saw pack and headed out, but Booth lingered. He touched her elbow. "Sure you're good?"

"I can handle this." She was aiming for confidence, but the worry lines etched into his forehead gave her pause. After he'd shared about being in WITSEC, she figured she owed him the truth. "It'll be tough, but if the wind eases back, and if you and Rico can contain the new fire, and if we can keep flames from running up the slope—"

"That's a lot of *ifs*."

"It's what we do." She didn't need to spell it out for him. Things had the potential to go big, especially if the fire on the north and south joined up.

He stepped closer. Brushed his index finger along her hand. "Be thinking about your escape route, okay?"

She pressed her lips into a tight smile and bobbed her head in short, rapid nods. "Always." What was she even agreeing to? Oh, yes. Escape plan. "There's a small cave to the west. Big enough for two of you."

"And you?"

"I'll squeeze in. If not, there's always my fire shelter." She patted her thigh pocket, where she kept the thin foil-like shelter she could deploy to protect herself in a fire. It was still risky, even as a last resort. They could only keep out so much heat, and even the smallest gap could mean death.

"Just remember, 'The sky, not the grave, is our goal.'"

Nova smiled at the line taken from an old hymn sung by their crew around the campfire.

She was about to respond when Rico yelled, "Booth! Stop playin' kissy-face and let's go!" Rico laughed and revved the chain saw.

"We'll talk after," she said. "Stay safe." She turned and headed off before she could change her mind and say or do something stupid.

Nova hoofed it across the valley and joined Eric. The treetops danced in the wind, waving fiery branches. Historical preservation was important, but not more than the lives of her crew. The fire was coming fast, and Nova wasn't sure they could stop it.

The radio crackled. "Burns, what's going on out there?"

She grabbed her unit. "Tuck, is that you?"

"Yep, I'm manning the command station. And before you ask, I've got my leg elevated and I'm fine."

Nova didn't blame the guy. It'd take a lot more than a broken leg to keep her out of a firefight. Especially one like this where the town was at risk. "It's worse than we thought. The fire's making a run up the slope on the south side. I don't think we can save these structures. The fire is about to blow up."

"Can you hold out another thirty? We can get you a full tanker to knock it down."

"Negative. At this point we don't have five minutes. We're going to backtrack and let the fire connect up on the left flank. Push it toward the river."

"We've got a chopper heading out to scout. Stay on this channel for updates."

"Ten-four." Nova wiped her sweaty cheek on the arm of her shirt. She turned to Eric. "Let's evac before this fire overruns us."

Eric lifted his gear with a bit of an old-man grunt. "Yeah…good idea. The wind's already dropping sparks onto the structures below."

Spot fires littered the dry grass on the hill behind the cabins—some the size of basketballs, others the size of her dining room table.

She saw a flash of movement from the main log cabin. From this distance, she could see a shadowy figure crouching.

A bear?

The figure stood and turned to face the window. Definitely a human.

"Hey! There's someone in there!" Nova took off running.

The fire raced down the hill behind the cabin. That old wooden structure was little more than tinder. Boots thudded the ground behind her, Eric hot on her heels.

"Hey! You there! The fire is coming! Get out now!"

The wind gusted, blowing red-hot debris into the valley. Embers fell on the shake-shingled roof. A burning tree toppled over and crashed through the window opening.

Nova lengthened her strides and hopped up on the front porch.

She dropped her PG bag on the porch and hit the door with her shoulder. The old wood cracked, and a rusted hinge let go.

All the glass in the windows had either deteriorated over time or been busted out. There was nothing to keep the smoke out. Red-orange fog filled the cabin.

Coughing, she dropped to her knees and crawled into the darkness. "Hey! Anyone here? Where are you?" She squinted through the smoke, trying to get her bearings. "Call out!"

The living room was littered with trash but otherwise empty of furnishings. The bedroom doors were straight ahead. Off to the right was a doorway leading to the kitchen with a see-through fireplace.

She heard Eric cough. "Eric! I'm going to the kitchen. Check the bedrooms. Our vic could be unconscious, unable to respond!"

"Affirm—" Eric coughed again.

Outside, the fire roared its hungry growl. Burning embers dropped on her back and neck from the bulging ceiling. Raging heat pressed in all around. She crawled through the kitchen door, splaying her hands and feeling for a body.

Her kneecap pressed down on something hard. It didn't quite register until she'd put all her weight on it. A sharp pain zipped through her knee and down her leg.

She looked down, expecting to see a rusty metal tool that would inevitably mean a tetanus shot. But it wasn't a tool or a can. It was a thick metal ring lying flat against the floor.

"Rico! Wait!" Nova heard Booth shout from outside.

Then a loud crash from behind. Someone cried out in pain.

"Rico! Are you okay?" Booth sounded frantic. "Talk to me, brother."

They needed her help. She crawled out of the kitchen. Where the front door had been was now darkness—the porch roof instead of an open exit. "Booth! What happened?"

"The porch collapsed on Rico. Oh man..." She heard banging and scratching that sounded like Booth digging.

Then he called out, "You and Eric need to get out of there now! The roof is about to come down!"

EIGHT

BOOTH DUG FOR RICO, PULLING BURNING HOT timbers off the pile and tossing them behind him.

"I'm here." Eric coughed. "I'm here. Go! Get Nova! I'll dig!"

"You left Nova inside?"

Eric tried to speak but started coughing again. He leaned over and braced his hands on his knees. The coughs came—raspy, hacking coughs that meant he had inhaled far too much smoke. The poor guy'd barely got himself out.

"I'll be right back." Booth handed him his water. "Nova! Can you crawl to the southeast window?"

"I'm all turned around," she yelled. "Go to the kitchen window!"

"Okay!" He didn't bother telling her that was the southeast. As he rounded the corner, Nova popped her head up, coughing and gasping. "It's okay. I got you."

"Someone...there was...someone...else." Nova's every word was followed by a cough.

He reached through the window and lifted her under the arms. She all but collapsed into him. He pulled her to his chest and dragged her over the windowsill. "See? I've always got your back."

When her feet hit the ground, she wobbled.

"Easy there. Give yourself a second. You breathed a lot of smoke."

"I...I'm..." Nova's eyes fluttered and rolled back.

He caught her before she fell, then lifted her into his arms. Her head lolled back and bounced as he hurried around front.

Eric, still coughing, had uncovered enough that Booth could see Rico's boot and part of his leg. And bone.

He lowered Nova to the ground and did a quick assessment.

Eric tossed a board aside. "She okay?"

"She's breathing. Strong pulse. I think it's smoke and heat inhalation." Booth ran over and grabbed one end of a beam. "She'll be fine, but we need an evac quick."

"You called?" Eric lifted the other end, and they laid the beam off to the side.

"I radioed for help." Booth's muscles screamed in protest, but he managed to move a broken support beam weighing down the other stuff on Rico. "We saw the fire jumping down the hill. Rico ran to help you guys, but the porch collapsed on top of him."

The heavy pounding of rotors filled the air.

"We've got incoming," Eric said.

Booth paused long enough to see the helicopter pass over and circle back, lining up the approach. He turned back and kept working to uncover Rico. "Help's here, buddy. Hang in there a few minutes longer."

Nova coughed. "Wh-what happened?"

Booth glanced over his shoulder. "You passed out."

"How'd I get out?" She worked herself into a sitting position. "Where's Eric?"

"Right here," Eric said with a cough. "Booth pulled you out and called for evac."

The helicopter set down in a field of sage brush as they pulled the last board off Rico. In a matter of minutes, the trauma team unloaded, and two men ran over with a basket to load the patient and heavy duffel bags.

Booth told them about the cave-in. "Rico has a pulse, but his leg is hurt bad. We didn't want to move him. Eric here breathed in a lot of smoke, but Nova the most. She was drowsy and confused when I pulled her out. Passed out a second later."

One of the medics shone a light in each of Nova's eyes. "Did you hit your head?"

"No," she coughed. "What happened to the person we saw in the cabin?"

Booth flicked a glance at Eric, who flattened his lips. "We never saw anyone else."

The trauma team extracted Rico. They placed him on a stretcher and ran to load him on the helicopter.

Booth and Eric packed up what little gear they could find. Moving slowly, Nova dug Rico's PG bag out of the rubble. A few minutes later, sweaty and out of breath, they climbed in beneath the turning helicopter rotors.

Once aboard, Booth sat next to Nova and buckled his seatbelt. "How you feeling?"

She lifted her oxygen mask. "Woozy but fine. Are they taking us back to the fire?"

He laughed. "You're joking, right? Rico is going to the hospital and so are you."

She squinted at him. "The town of Snowhaven is at risk, Booth." Nova's words were stuttered with coughing. "Who knows how big the fire is now? Three thousand acres? We need to be in there."

Stubborn woman. They could've been killed, and she was ready for more.

All he could do was placate her for now. "I know. So put your mask on and let's get you cleared to go back to work."

"Fine." She pulled the oxygen mask over her nose and mouth, crossed her arms and looked away.

The sun sank low in the hazy sky, setting the whole landscape alight in a fiery orange glow. In a cloud of dust and flying debris, the helicopter lifted clear of the ground.

Booth stared out the window. Below, the fire rolled like a wave over the historical mining claim they'd been sent to save.

The fire that might have cost Nova her life if Booth hadn't been there.

Nova inhaled a long, slow breath and promptly started coughing. She closed her eyes, but all she saw was Booth beside her, determined to be her hero.

"Looks like all the burns are first-degree. I've prescribed some topical antibiotic ointment, but I imagine you have loads of it at home already." The doctor, who'd introduced herself as Dr. Zamudio, flipped her stethoscope over her head and let it drop around her shoulders. "We're going to need a chest X-ray to check your lungs for smoke damage. You were pretty lethargic when you came in."

"How long is that going to take?" Nova scissor-kicked her legs on the edge of the table. The white sanitary paper crinkled.

"We're backed up. Could be an hour."

"An hour!" Nova knew that meant two or three. She'd already had the few burns treated.

"You wildland firefighters crack me up." Dr. Zamudio simpered—a closemouthed, high-pitched laugh that gave her a girlish quality. "Girl, you ever heard of 'rescuer safety first'? You're no good to nobody if you collapse out there in the woods. Your buddies don't need to be worrying about you while they face a fire themselves neither."

Dr. Zamudio was right, more than she probably knew. But Nova couldn't tell her just how bad things were out there. They were calling in teams from Alaska and Canada to come and help. News like that would cause a panic. Better to let an evacuation order come down from forestry service.

"You all come in here smellin' like a backyard barbecue and expect doctors to slap a Band-aid on your burns and send you back out there. Uh-hum." The black bun on top of her head wobbled when she shook her head. "Not good enough."

"Okay, I get it. Can I at least go check on Rico, see how he's doing?" The rookie smokejumper was her responsibility.

"Because my staff want to chase you down all over the hospital when it's time for your test?" The doctor's brow furrowed. "You don't need to go on a wild-hog chase. He's headed to surgery, hon."

It was worse than Nova realized. She'd seen the

open fracture where the bone stuck out of Rico's shin. Thinking of it sent chills up her spine. "That bad?"

The doc held up an index finger, then used the same finger to slide her clear-framed glasses up her nose. "Now, you know I can't go telling you his medical information until he signs a release. Unless you're his next of kin, of course."

Nova shook her head. "There's a release in his file. We all have them so you can give status updates on our condition in emergencies."

Dr. Zamudio nodded and walked to the rolling computer cart.

Her fingers clacked the keyboard. She paused and pushed her glasses up her nose again. "Mm-hmm. Mm-hmm. Okay."

Nova swung her leg, hitting the back of her boot on the table.

Dr. Zamudio clicked the mouse around, then used a keystroke combo to lock the computer. "So, I see I can give you updates. I'm sorry, but your friend Mr. Torres has multiple fractures and a collapsed lung. We have him listed as critical."

Nova caught her lower lip between her teeth while she considered the words. Rico could've been killed trying to save her. Shoot, Eric could've been killed—her too. All because she'd tried to save someone who wasn't even there.

But they *had* been there. She'd seen them with her own two eyes.

There was a light knock on the door. A woman in scrubs peeked in. "I'm Stephanie. Here to take Miss Burns to radiology."

"Oh, look at that. They're moving faster than I

thought." Dr. Zamudio patted Nova's knee and winked. "She's all yours."

Stephanie smiled. "Okay, if you'll follow me Nova."

Nova followed the nurse through a maze of corridors, wondering if the doctor had done that on purpose. Told her it would be an hour just to get a rise out of her. She did want to go see Rico, but where was Booth? Probably checking on Crispin.

She still couldn't believe Booth was a federal agent living in hiding.

He should've picked a job that didn't require him to drop everything at a moment's notice to run and fight wildfires if what he wanted to do was solve his case.

Whatever the case was anyway.

"Here we are." Stephanie held the door to radiology open.

Thirty minutes later, nurse Stephanie led Nova back to her room. The sound of her boots squeaking with each step was drowned out by shouting. It sounded like Booth.

At the next hallway intersection, Stephanie turned left, but Nova turned right.

Stephanie followed Nova. "Your room is this way."

"I know. Thanks. I can find it from here." She coughed. "I need to talk to my friend."

At the end of the hall, Booth gripped the nurses' station with both hands.

"Where is he?" His neck flushed red up to his jawline.

Nova hurried over. "Hey, what's wrong? Who are you looking for?"

Booth looked at her for a full beat, as if surprised to see her standing there. "Crispin. He's not in his room."

"Maybe they took him for some tests."

"No!" His voice clicked up in volume. "That's what I'm saying. They lost him! They said he was here this morning, but when they went to do rounds, he was gone. I don't understand how they can lose a patient."

Nova slipped her hand around his arm and pulled him to face her. "Hey, yelling isn't going to do anything except disturb the other patients and get you kicked out of here. You got your phone back from Houston, right?"

Booth nodded.

"Good. Let's leave your number with the nurse. She can call you if Crispin turns up. Meanwhile, take me to his room, and we'll see if he left a note or something."

Booth worked his jaw, then nodded. He turned back to the nurse. "Look, I apologize for being rude. Do you have something I can write my number on?"

The nurse pushed a blank piece of paper toward him and dropped a pen on the counter. Booth clicked the pen open and scribbled his digits. "Sorry. Please call me if you see him."

She looked unconvinced but nodded.

Nova took Booth's hand as he led her to Crispin's room. Inside, she let go of Booth and closed the door.

The hospital room was the basic setup. Closet. Bathroom. Hospital bed with the sheets tossed back. A blue-green couch underlining the windows on the far wall. Booth was right. Crispin wasn't here.

"Is it possible Crispin just walked out of here?"

She pretty much cringed as the words came out. It sounded stupid. The man had a gunshot wound.

Booth was pulling out the drawers on the nightstand. "Sounds like him. Could he really unhook his monitors and walk off without the medical staff knowing?"

"I saw a patient in a wheelchair, sitting outside with her IV pole and smoking a cigarette." She shrugged.

He walked to the closet and peered inside. "His clothes are gone." Booth crossed the room and sat on the couch.

She sat beside him and rested her forearms on her knees, matching his posture. "Were you being serious about…you know…WITSEC?"

He didn't look up but twisted his hands. "Yeah."

"How long?"

"Three years."

"You left everything behind? Your friends? Family?"

He nodded.

"Were you…married?"

He breathed a short laugh. "Nope. Never married. No kids. Not many friends in the job I had either. The team here is the closest I've had to friends in a long time."

"What about Crispin?"

"He was dead. We were partners, and I thought he'd been killed."

And then he'd seen his friend, back from the dead, right here in Booth's town. Nova couldn't imagine what that might feel like.

"The rogue CIA faction. Hillbilly militia. Terrorists. Crazy Henry…" She looked at him.

"They're not made-up stories to tell around the campfire, are they?"

He shook his head. "It all happened. I might have changed a few names here and there, but the events are real."

"Okay, but a military dog who needed a bodyguard from some guy making chemical warfare bombs?" She gave him the side-eye. "Come on. That's got to be embellished, right?"

"Nope. That dog is still considered a high-value target to this day."

Nova sat back and pulled one leg underneath her. "Will you tell me how you ended up here? As a smokejumper?"

"Okay, let me think where to start. The entire team was under suspicion because someone was feeding intel to a rogue CIA faction about the location of a missing nuke. Everybody was pointing fingers at everyone else, so Henry planned an off-the-books takedown meant to draw out the mole. At the last minute, I got a call that my mother had suffered a cardiac episode and had to go to the hospital."

"Oh no."

"It turned out to be an artery blockage. While I was at the hospital with her, they moved forward with the takedown. The whole operation went wrong somehow. There was a huge explosion that supposedly killed Crispin." His thumb traced the red scrapes over his knuckles. "I knew everyone would point fingers at me. I mean, Crispin's dead, Henry's disappeared, and the nuke is nowhere to be found. Nobody knew who the mole really was."

Nova nodded. "And you were the last man standing?"

"Right." Booth scratched his beard. "I was still at the hospital with Mom, planning to confront the supervisors the next day and explain why I wasn't at the takedown. I wanted to help figure out who was responsible for my friend dying in the explosion.

"A delivery messenger came to the hospital and handed me a manila envelope," he continued. "Inside was a note saying that when I walked back into work, I'd be labeled a terrorist and charged with treason. Possibly killed."

"You'd be the scapegoat," Nova added. She was starting to see how complicated this case really was and why Booth was so invested.

"The note said I should go into hiding here in Ember and wait for Henry to contact me. It was a part of the failsafe plan Henry'd had all along."

It was starting to make sense. Booth was hiding out, waiting for his redemption. "Something I can't quite figure out is why you became a smokejumper."

"I was a volunteer wildland firefighter in high school, helitack crew in college, then parachute infantry in the Army." Booth shrugged. "I needed a job."

She'd heard of worse reasons.

It occurred to her that if he was in WITSEC, then he probably had a false identity. "Is your name really Booth Wilder?"

He angled to face her. "It is now. The old me is legally dead. I was given a new identity and sent here."

"That would be so…I don't know." She leaned forward. Ran her thumb over the soft bristles of his beard. Heard him swallow.

If Sophie hadn't interrupted them, Nova would've

kissed Booth right there by the horses. She'd imagined it. Tried to talk herself out of it. Even avoided him so she wouldn't be tempted. Other people might not know who Booth was, but she was pretty sure that she did.

"You know..." Her eyes dropped to his lips. Lingered. "I've never kissed a stranger before."

Booth leaned in. "There's a first time for everything." His voice was low.

A shiver tingled down her spine. "I've never been one to back down from a challenge."

"Why stop now?" He slipped his hand around the back of her neck and hesitated.

Nova waited, the soft warmth of his lips a sliver away.

The air between them sizzled.

She couldn't stand it anymore. Nova tilted her head and kissed him. Her hands went up to cup his jaw, pulling him closer for a lengthy kiss.

Everything she hadn't said but wanted to, everything she wanted to ask him but hadn't—it all passed between them in that moment.

The trill of a cell phone drew them apart. They both reached for their phones.

Booth was on his feet. He found a flip phone in his front pocket. "It's Crispin." He snapped it open and put it to his ear. "Where are—"

His whole body stiffened.

"I swear, if you—" He pulled the phone away and stared at the screen. Snapped it closed and stuffed it in his pocket.

Nova crossed the room to stand beside him. "Who was that?"

"The man who has Crispin. He wants to meet, but

he has some demands for an exchange." He turned and started to leave.

"Where are you going?"

"To save Crispin and get my life back."

Nova stepped in front of him. "Wait, you can't leave. It could be a trap. Let the police—"

"I am the police," he said.

Then it dawned on her. "You never cared about this team from the beginning. You were just here to live out your giant lie."

Booth took a step back as if her words had physically shoved him. "Yeah, well, if I didn't have to always watch your back, then I would have been able to solve this long ago."

Nova stood there and watched him walk out the door. Her fingers touched her lips. Part of her couldn't blame him.

He wanted to save his friend and maybe save the world.

Start a new life.

One that didn't include her.

NINE

PERFECT. JUST PERFECT. BOOTH HAD FINALLY LET himself open up to Nova—finally broken through her defenses—and now he had to walk away? Stupid. No way would she take him back when he finally finished all this and showed up.

Begging for forgiveness.

Okay, but wow. He hadn't expected that kiss. He'd wanted to kiss her, sure. Just...hadn't expected it.

Now he had to go rescue Crispin and end this with the taste of Nova on his lips. So sweet. But walking away was nothing but bitter.

Which meant he had limited time to get to jump base and find his gun.

But first, he needed to find a ride.

He jogged down the stairs and through the halls until he found the nurses' station in the ER.

"I'm looking for Eric Dale. He's with the Jude County Smokejumpers."

"Just released." The nurse didn't bother to look up. She pointed to the exit door with her pen. "If you hurry, you might be able to catch him."

Booth slapped his palm on the Formica counter. "Thanks."

Why was he forced to choose between his old life and this new one? He knew the reason.

He couldn't let Crispin die. Couldn't let the bad guys win any more than he could let a fire destroy a town. He'd already lost Crispin once. Thought his friend was dead and gone. He couldn't go through that again. The town needed him, but there were twenty-plus wildland firefighters working on it, with more to come. Who did Crispin have?

No one.

He pushed through the exit door into the parking garage, where he saw Eric walking arm in arm with his wife, Shelly.

He jogged over to him. "Hey, man, how you feeling?"

Eric held up his bandaged forearm. "Pretty good hot spot on my arm. I could probably work, but the doc is worried about infection."

"And you're going to listen to him this time." Shelly was a pretty brunette, petite enough to fit in the crook of Eric's arm. They had three children under the age of ten and lived in Ember to be close to Eric during fire season.

"Aw, Shelly knows I could've kept it covered and gone back to work. She just wants me home. You watch. She'll have a honey-do list a mile long. My arm won't be an excuse then."

Shelly nudged him in the ribs. "You know I stopped waiting around for you and started on the list myself. Anyway, Booth, how's Nova and Rico?"

"Nova's good. I think she'll be released to work

today. Rico...well, he's not so hot, but the doc is optimistic about the surgery."

"He's tough," Eric said.

Booth nodded. "I think he'll pull through, but he's out for the season."

Eric scratched at the bandage on his arm. "What about you? Headed back to the line?"

"Yeah, but I have something to take care of first. I was hoping you could give me a ride to jump base so I can pick something up."

"Sure we can. Right, honey?" Eric looked to Shelly.

"Of course. We're parked right over here."

Eric and Shelly had quiet marriage talk in the front seat. Booth leaned against the window and tried to come up with a plan.

Whoever had taken Crispin had made a huge mistake. His past was calling, and Booth was more than ready to answer.

Shelly pulled into the lot of jump base and parked.

Booth leaned up and patted Eric's shoulder. "Thanks for the lift. Feel better."

"Stay safe, brother."

Booth got out and walked around the construction dumpster. Much of the front of the building had been demolished over the last few days, clearing out the charred remains of the structure so it could be built anew.

Funny, considering that's what he needed to do with his life.

He was ready for a fresh start. Booth wanted to see where things went with Nova, if she'd give him another shot. First, he had to rip out the charred remains of his old life once and for all. He could decide how to rebuild from there.

Go back to work in Homeland? Leave behind Jude County and smokejumping? Risk losing Nova forever? It was all too much to think about now.

The burner phone rang and Booth answered. "Talk."

"Bring Henry Snow to me," the man said.

"I keep trying to tell you, I don't know where he is," Booth said, walking inside. How would he know where his boss had been all these years?

"You're lyin'. You and Crispin are here to protect him. How about this? You bring Snow to me, and I'll think about lettin' you live." He horked a coughing laugh.

Booth started to deny the accusation, but it could work in his favor. Pretend to exchange Crispin for Snow.

He ducked under the restricted tape and ran to the ready room. "Look, I'll bring Snow, but I'm not doing anything until I know Crispin is okay."

The call disconnected.

Booth stopped by his locker and stared at the phone. Had he made a mistake? Pushed too hard?

The phone chimed with an incoming text.

Booth clicked it and saw a blurry photo of Crispin lying on a bare mattress on the floor. The bandage wrapped around his shoulder showed dried blood spots. Crispin's eyes were closed, his good arm handcuffed to the leg of a cast-iron wood stove.

When the phone rang, Booth answered it. "Not good enough. He could be dead in that picture."

The caller growled. "What do you suggest?"

"Tell me where you are. I'll come to you."

There was silence on the other end. Finally, he said, "Give me ten minutes. I'll text the location. Bring Snow or Crispin will die."

"It's going to take some time."

The call ended.

Booth shoved the phone back into his pocket and pulled a small metal box out of his locker. He put his hand in the grooves and waited for the fingerprint scanner to read his prints. There was a whirring sound as the mechanical lock released.

The lid squeaked open and he found his weapon there in a paddle holster. He clipped it inside his waistband and concealed it with his shirt. The cold weight of an extra magazine settled in his leg pocket.

Booth was sprinting for the airplane hangar, where he kept his motorcycle, when his burner phone chimed again.

A text with an address popped up.

He'd expected to be sent deep into the state forest, but the location was just north of Ember.

He cranked up the motorcycle and backed out of the hangar. His back tire kicked up gravel and he sped off.

Twenty minutes later, he turned off the rural route onto the narrow dirt road crowded with towering pines that needed to be cut back.

He rolled to a stop, cut the engine, and pushed his bike into the trees. Some brush coverage meant it wouldn't be seen from the road.

Booth weaved his way through the woods on foot, boots crunching on dead pine needles. Each step crackled as loud as gunfire in his ears. He ducked between the weathered trunks, seeking, searching.

Crispin was here somewhere, being held against his will.

Or worse.

Booth clenched his teeth. He couldn't lose his friend again.

He drew his gun out of the holster and clicked the safety off. Pulled the slide back enough to see the glint of brass in the chamber.

Up ahead, a small rustic cabin was nestled in a stand of pines, a beat-up old pickup truck parked beside it. A muddy four-wheeler sat in the front yard. Upended logs encircled a campfire ring on the opposite side of the yard. The woodsy smell of a still-smoldering fire permeated the area.

Someone had been here not long ago.

Easing back into the brush's camouflage, Booth picked his way through the trees until he was beside the truck. He checked the cab. Empty.

Trash filled the truck bed. Crushed beer cans, an old shovel, fast-food wrappers, sandbags probably left over from winter, and a metal gas can.

Booth crept around the cabin and peered in the back window. Crispin lay unmoving on a ratty mattress. Just like with the photo, Booth couldn't tell if he was unconscious or dead. Then he saw it. The slow rise and fall of his chest.

For now, Crispin was alive.

In the cabin's small kitchen, a man with a sloped forehead and small coal-black eyes poured coffee into a chipped mug. A chain hung from his leather belt. He'd cut the sleeves off his T-shirt to expose the tattoos up and down his arms. Military bearing. Confident. Dangerous.

Floyd Blackwell.

Booth gritted his teeth. Eyes narrowed, he scanned the silent cabin once more. Floyd and Crispin were alone.

Booth sneaked back to the truck and crouched beside the front tire. His jaw ticked as a plan took shape.

He had an idea.

A dangerous one.

The roar of the airplane engines did nothing to drown out Nova's pulse pounding in her ears. She was so dumb.

She'd taken a huge risk. Opened herself to the idea of falling for Booth. Laid it all on the line, and he'd left her standing there holding her heart in her hands.

And could she even blame him?

The man was saving the world.

"Hey, kid." Aria's voice came over Nova's headset. "Come chat for a sec."

Nova picked her way to the cockpit, stepping over the other jumpers and scooting around the cargo. The plane was stuffed tight with six new guys in from Alaska. They'd flown in to assist before the fire reached the small town of Snowhaven. Finn and Nova were the only smokejumpers from Jude County who weren't either out with an injury or already out on the fire line.

Except Booth.

Who knew where he was?

Once Dr. Zamudio had cleared her to go back to work, Nova had tried to track him down, but her calls and texts went unanswered. That was nothing new. Booth was the worst at answering his phone. The crew needed his help, but the fire wouldn't wait. So she'd loaded up and headed to do what she did best. Wildfire fighting.

Nova ducked into the cockpit and sat in the empty copilot seat. She buckled in and took in the view. White-capped mountains and rolling green hills spread out as far as she could see. "Wow."

"Best seat in the house." Aria gave her a long look that made the hair on the back of her neck prickle. "Except something's going on with you."

Nova picked at a callus on her thumb. "I'm just annoyed, that's all."

"Booth isn't here. You're storming around being short with everyone." Aria tapped her finger to her temple. "I'm a smart cookie. I can put the two together. What's up?"

She wasn't that transparent. Aria just knew her better than anyone else. Nova couldn't give her the full story, but she had to give her something. "I kissed Booth."

Aria's eyes went wide. "And?"

"And...nothing." She folded her arms. "He's not here."

"So, nothing has got you all bristled?" She flashed a look of disbelief. "For real. Out with it."

Fine. Venting to Aria always seemed to help, and she'd end up telling her at some point. "We were at the hospital and started talking. I don't know what came over me, but...I kissed him." She smiled at the memory. The warmth of his lips. The strength of his hands around her shoulders. A moment where she'd felt safe. But it had been over before it'd started. "He took a call and had to rush off."

"He didn't say why?"

Nova shook her head. "It was clear the call was important, but...I don't know." If she were honest, she was mad at herself for feeling something.

"Wow, I can't believe *you* kissed *him*. Bold. Way to go. I'm proud of you, girl." She reached over and patted her thigh. "So...how was it?"

Nova's face betrayed her with a big goofy grin. "Fantastic."

Aria smiled. She flipped a switch and radioed the fire boss to let them know they'd be approaching in twenty minutes. "So are you guys a couple now?"

"No, and I don't think we ever will be. Relationships are too complicated. Sure, it was nice, but it's got me all distracted. You know that's a problem for jumpers."

"Speaking of—you guys should start your buddy checks. We're dealing with erratic winds, and things are gonna be rough."

"That high north wind is blowing the fires together." Nova released her buckle and stood hunched in the cockpit. "We'll get it, but say a prayer for us."

"Always," Aria said.

Nova crawled back to the stone-faced Alaskan jumpers, and minutes later, the plane descended to work out the pattern for the drop. The spotter pulled open the door, and the air roared in. Nova and the other jumpers did their equipment checks while the spotter assessed conditions.

After the streamers, the spotter turned to Nova and Finn with a rather grim look on his face. "It looks pretty bad, but I think you can handle it. Just don't land between the fires. With all the smoke, you won't be able to see where you're going. If things get tricky, go long, and stay wide of the bluff. Last thing we need is one of you falling off a cliff."

Nova glanced at Finn, who was securing his gear with a deep crease between his brows. Something in his demeanor seemed off today. "You good?" she asked over the roar of the propellers.

Finn gave a curt nod, not quite meeting her gaze. Before she could question him further, the spotter yelled for them to get in the door.

The afternoon sun streaked crimson across the smoke-filled sky. Nova dropped into the open door. Her heart hammered in her chest, but she lived for these moments.

The spotter gave her the slap, and she pushed off, tumbling out into space at ninety miles an hour. She tracked away from the plane, giving Finn plenty of room as she tried to orient herself. Descending into the smoke, she got shoved west, then north by the wind.

The world spun around her, and Nova lost the jump spot. "Blast it!"

After counting off the seconds, she pulled her ripcord and got flung back up when the canopy deployed. Wind swirled around the head of the main fire, playing havoc with all sense of control, dragging her like she was nothing. No strength to fight it. No control.

She pulled hard on the toggles, trying to spill air from the chute and slow her descent. But nothing could stop her helpless trajectory toward the towering Douglas firs.

She couldn't see a thing except how close she was to the enormous treetops.

A blood-curdling shout pierced the roaring wind.

Nova jerked her gaze upward to see Finn hurtling straight toward her. His undeployed chute streamed uselessly above him.

Before she could even suck in a breath to scream, Finn crashed into her billowing canopy.

Nova's chute collapsed. Tangled together, they fell in an uncontrolled plunge.

"Finn!" They spun in free fall. "Reserve! Reserve!"

Finn's body hung limp. His chin lolling on his chest.

"Finn! Finn!" Nova screamed to no avail. "Wake up! Pull your reserve!"

Air buffeted them as they rocketed toward the trees on the ground, standing in rows like spears of an invading army. They needed to separate somehow, or they'd both die.

Finn was still unconscious. Nova had no choice but to get free on her own and pray the automatic activation device deployed his reserve. If it didn't, she would be saving herself and condemning him to death.

Knots drew tight in her stomach. She clawed at Finn's rig, managing to yank his cut-away handle to jettison his main chute.

"Reserve, Finn!" she shrieked one last time.

Gritting her teeth, she yanked her own cutaway handle. Slipped. Caught on the lines. Kicked and struggled until she fell away.

Nova's pulse hammered. She activated her emergency reserve. Felt the crack of it inflating. The familiar tug of her parachute unfurling. The canopy caught and slowed her descent.

In the same heartbeat, she glimpsed Finn still hurtling, deadweight, toward the jagged trees below.

"No! Oh, God! Finn! Fiiiinn!" Why wasn't his AAD working?

Time was running out. If it didn't deploy soon—oh, God, help him.

Like an answer to her frenzied prayers, his automated backup kicked in, cracking open mere feet above the raging inferno below. Finn's battered body soared over a stand of burning firs and disappeared into the swirling smoke.

Tears streamed down her face.

Gasping, she maneuvered her parachute away from the flames. What had she done? Why had she cut away?

She knew why. It was the protocol for entanglements. Still...she'd tried to save them both. Instead, she'd almost certainly caused Finn's death.

Nova choked back a sob. She had to focus or she'd suffer the same fate. After wiping a tear, she turned her attention to navigating toward a clearing on the edge of the burn.

The wind continued to drive the fire. Flames roared at the edge of the drop zone, thrusting waves of blistering air upward and wreaking havoc with her ability to control the descent.

This landing was not going to be pretty.

She fought to tame the bucking parachute as she neared the treetops, aiming for a slender gap in the fire. A sudden thermal grabbed the canopy, dragging Nova sideways despite all her efforts. The wind propelled her over the brink of a sheer rock face concealed by the dense smoke.

Nova spilled every bit of air possible from her chute in an attempt to stall her forward movement as she lost altitude. But the merciless updraft shoved her out over what she could now see was a treacherous canyon glowing red with advancing flames below. Facing the horrifying prospect of being dumped into the inferno, she cut away the last of her rigging just as it dragged her over the precipice.

Her breath caught as she braced herself for impact.

A scream tore from her throat as she plunged toward the canyon floor. She clawed at crumbling shale, her nails tearing, finding no purchase on the frictionless grade. A sharp pain tore through the sleeve of her fire shirt. She tumbled down and slammed onto a narrow ledge.

Her helmet cracked against stone.

Nova slid over the edge.

TEN

Booth leaned the shovel against a tree and wiped the sweat from his forehead. He'd taken about fifteen minutes to dig a six-inch-wide fire line in an arc.

He grabbed the red gas can he'd taken from the truck. The reek of gasoline permeated his nostrils as he splashed the line of vegetation bordering the cabin. He trailed back into the woods, soaking the blanket of pine needles and desiccated brush. The perfect fuse.

Next, he took a burning stick from the campfire ring and knelt in the woods. Watching. Waiting.

It seemed like forever before Floyd exited the cabin, coffee mug in hand. "Where is he?" He held a cell phone up to the sky. "Dern spotty cell coverage."

Booth held his breath and touched the flaming stick to the gasoline-soaked trail.

The line ignited with a soft whump.

Flames chewed through the fuel. Smoke boiled up in noxious plumes as the fire found more vegetation to consume.

"What the—" Floyd jumped back. His mug

shattered on the ground, spilling his drink. He bolted inside under a stream of expletives.

Booth was already on the move, circling wide along the blaze toward the truck parked in front.

Floyd exploded from the cabin with a rifle in his hand. "Hey! Who's out there!" He stumbled off the porch, coughing. "If that's you, Wilder, your friend is going to die. Same way my brother did!"

Booth burst from cover, his pistol aimed at Floyd's chest. "Drop it, Floyd! Hands up or you'll never take another breath!"

Floyd's face twisted into a snarl. His hand twitched to raise his rifle.

"Don't even think about it." Booth took a step toward Floyd.

Ten feet separated them.

"I knew you'd come running. Always gotta be the hero. You and that friend of yours. Casper."

"Crispin." Booth took another step.

Eight feet.

Floyd snorted. "Casper's a better name. Especially after I'm through with him."

"Last chance. Put your gun down. I don't want to shoot you." He closed another step.

Six feet.

"Go ahead! Shoot me! Do it! What are you waiting for!" Floyd sneered.

Booth took a step closer.

Five feet.

Apparently, that hadn't been coffee in Floyd's cup, because Booth could smell alcohol on his breath. "I'm warning you, Floyd. Put the rifle down."

"You ain't an agent no more. You're a smokejumper who don't have the guts to shoot."

Little did he know, Booth did have the guts to shoot. In fact, his finger clenched tighter around the trigger, ready to squeeze. "Put. Down. Your. Weapon."

Floyd lunged. With a garbled shout, he swung the rifle at Booth's head.

Booth dodged. Wasn't fast enough. Agonizing stars exploded as the stock cracked against his shoulder. Shooting pain screamed up his arm. He stumbled but held the gun steady on Floyd's chest, trigger finger itching to fire.

Floyd's rifle went up fast.

A deafening crack split the chaos.

Booth flinched but the shot went wild.

He charged Floyd. Together they crashed backward. The rifle hit the ground, and Booth kicked it away. Floyd scrambled to his feet and ran for his truck, fumbling for the gun in his waistband.

Two shots rang out.

Booth dove behind a tree as bullets bit into the bark.

A gust of wind blew burning debris onto the porch. Embers found the liquid from Floyd's coffee cup and burst into flames. The wooden planks caught. In seconds, the narrow porch was engulfed in flames.

No, no, no. Crispin was in there!

Booth popped up and returned fire.

The first went wide, but his second shot exploded the rear window of Floyd's truck.

"You'll pay for this!" Floyd bellowed. He squeezed off another wild shot and hopped onto the ATV.

The engine growled and Floyd gunned it. He

drove straight through the fire, headed for the woods behind the cabin.

Booth squeezed off a couple more shots after him but only managed to pepper the ground as Floyd disappeared into the woods.

His prime suspect. Gone.

But his partner could still be alive.

Booth jumped over the burning porch and burst through the cabin door. He braced for an attack. Only silence greeted him. Inside the dingy interior, he smelled the metallic tang of blood.

From the mattress in the corner, Crispin lifted his head. "What took you so long?" The words came out cracked and hoarse.

Even from across the room, Booth could see he was in rough shape. Crispin's arms and face were mottled black and blue with contusions. "You should've stayed in the hospital. Anyone else here?"

Crispin winced. "Don't think so, but that greasy dude who shot me was here earlier."

Booth hadn't seen anyone in the cabin with Floyd, but he swept the two cramped rooms with his gun leading the way. Empty.

"Now that you've had the tour, think you can uncuff me?" Crispin rattled the handcuffs.

Holstering his weapon, Booth went to Crispin. "I don't suppose you have the key?"

"Nope."

"I'm guessing a bobby pin is too much to ask for."

"Best I can offer is that pair of sunglasses over there." Crispin tipped his head toward the table, where a pair of aviators sat.

"That'll work." Booth broke off the metal earpiece and used it to pick the lock on the cuff around

Crispin's wrist. After about fifteen seconds, it disengaged with a click. "We need to move fast. You okay to walk?"

Crispin nodded and eased into a sitting position. "Why do we have to move fast?"

"I sorta set the cabin on fire." His eyes landed on a set of keys tossed atop a nearby crate. Floyd's ride, no doubt. God seemed to be on their side for once.

"You what?" Crispin shouted. "Are you nuts? You coulda killed me!"

Booth snatched the keys. "In my defense, I only set the grass on fire. The wind blew the fire onto the porch." Aware Floyd could return at any moment, Booth headed for the door. "We can discuss it later. Let's go."

Crispin tried to get to his feet. He groaned and fell back on the mattress.

"I got you, buddy." With as much care as he could muster, Booth lifted Crispin to his feet. He pulled Crispin's good arm around his shoulder and wrapped an arm around his friend's waist.

Somehow, Booth managed to stay upright and stagger through the fire without scoring major burns for either of them. He half carried Crispin to the battered pickup just outside.

At the sight of Floyd's vehicle, Booth breathed a sigh.

They might just make it out of here alive after all.

Nova's heart thundered in her ears, drowning out the growing crackle of advancing flames. Biting back a scream, she staggered deeper into the woods, clutching her broken ribs with one arm. She'd survived that horrific midair collision with Finn, but the fire had her trapped on the mountainside with no way out.

If she was going down, she wouldn't go easy. Not Nova Burns.

Her ankle screamed with each step, but she limped onward. Smoke stung her eyes, making it impossible to orient herself or judge the fire's proximity. There had to be something she could do. Some way out.

All she'd wanted was to follow in her uncle Jock's footsteps. It had been her driving purpose since before she could carry a Pulaski. Oh, she was following in his footsteps all right. Facing an excruciating end by being overrun by a fire.

What good was that lifelong dream if she died alone?

Booth's face flashed in her mind. His floppy hair and wide grin stirred an ache in her heart. If only they'd had more time to explore the spark igniting between them. But it was too late for regrets.

A high-pitched mewl stopped Nova in her tracks.

She squinted into the haze. Wide eyes peered out of the brush near the base of a tree. Nova recognized the round ears and mottled coat.

A mountain lion cub.

And where there was a cub, its ferociously protective mother wouldn't be far behind.

As if on cue, a blood-chilling growl rumbled behind her.

Adrenaline spiked through Nova's battered body. She made a slow, awkward turn on her twisted ankle.

A sleek and powerful female mountain lion stared

at Nova. Her ears were pinned back. Body crouched low to the ground. Hindquarters raised. Tail twitching.

"Okay, mama. I'm a human, not dinner." She kept eye contact and spoke in a loud, assertive voice. "You stay there. I'll leave you and your baby alone."

Too bad she didn't have a frozen steak in her leg pocket today. Or maybe it was a good thing.

She began backing up. Slow and easy. She didn't dare turn her back.

The cub's cries sharpened.

"Go! Go take care of your baby! Go on!" Nova waved her arms. "Get outta here before the fire—"

The soil dissolved beneath her boots, and she was swallowed up by darkness.

A scream lodged in her throat.

Arms windmilling, she grappled for something to stop her fall.

Nova landed hard on crumbling shafts of wood. The planks under her back gave way, and she careened down a rough slope. Jagged splinters pierced her skin and snagged her uniform. She tumbled over a staggered wooden barrier and slid to a stop.

Nova planted her hands and pushed off the ground, forcing herself to sit. She spat rotted sawdust into the dirt beside her. Every breath sent shards of stabbing pain through her ribs. She had to suck air between her teeth just to get her mind to quit spinning.

Nova looked around, but all she saw was darkness and the faint shadows of the pile of rubble that had collapsed in.

She was trapped.

Buried alive.

She fumbled for the tiny flashlight in her pocket. Her hands shook but she managed to drag it out. A flick of the switch yielded no light. She banged it on her palm. Really? Nothing?

"Blast!" She threw the useless thing against the wall, and the clattering sound echoed into the darkness.

Breathe, just breathe...

Wait. Didn't miners die breathing toxic gasses in caves?

Stop. Just...stop.

There were tunnels and caves all over these mountains. Surely she could find her way out of here.

She scanned the shadowy outlines of rocky debris blocking the way back. No way could she dig through that barricade with her injuries. Even if she had the strength, those unstable mine workings could collapse and crush her.

Which left her with only one choice.

Face the unknown darkness—pray for another exit.

Nova crawled to the nearest wall and dragged herself upright. Her head swam, and she had to brace a hand to stay upright on unsteady legs while she fought the encroaching unconsciousness.

"Easy...easy does it."

She put one boot in front of the other. Forced herself to keep going. One crumbling passage then another. More than once she freaked herself out, thinking she'd heard scratching or boots splashing in water.

"Hey! Who goes there?" A man's voice echoed through the tunnel.

Nova jumped, sending pain tearing through her body. White stars cluster-bombed her vision.

She had to be hallucinating.

A beam of light swept the floor in front of her. Less than twenty feet away stood the outline of a hulking figure.

Her instinct was to curl up in a little ball and hide. She'd faced down a mountain lion, but she didn't have any more fight in her.

"I...I'm sorry—" Her voice came out hoarse.

"Speak up!" the figure bellowed. "Who are you, and what'n blazes are you doing in my cave?"

Nova swallowed. A hot tear rolled down her cheek. "I—I fell through a shaft and I'm hurt—" The lump in her throat made it hard to speak "My name is Nova. I didn't mean to intrude. There was a fire and a mountain lion..."

"Sounds like you've been through a lot." The man walked closer, his face illuminated by the flashlight. Bearded, with wild tufts of white hair, the old man looked downright grandfatherly. "Nice to finally meet you, Nova. Name's Henry."

Nova's heart skipped a beat. No...okay...yes. She was definitely hallucinating. "Figures. I did hit my head. You're not real." She sagged against the wall. "Of course I think of you now. Probably because of Booth."

"Who's that?"

"This guy on my team. He was a Homeland Security agent and tells all these stories about a man named Crazy Henry that he says are all true." Hope trembled in that single cracked word.

The old man straightened, then chuckled. "My reputation precedes me. Can't say I get many visitors." His brow furrowed. "In fact, I discourage it."

"Crazy Henry! Booth was right." She rasped an incredulous laugh that morphed to coughing. "You see, there was a fire. At the smokejumper base. I had to save this woman, but then Booth had to save me. And then he saw the guy who set the fire, and they fought, but he escaped. Then Booth went to meet his friend Crispin, and some other guy had beat him up then shot him. So we got a helicopter to take Crispin to the hospital so we could fight a wildfire. And before we go, Booth tells me he's not really even a smokejumper. He's a Homeland agent."

Nova realized the words were pouring out, but she couldn't stop herself. "Then we tried to save this mining camp, and I saw someone in a cabin. But the cabin collapsed and we almost died. And Crispin walked right out of the hospital. But some man called Booth saying he had Crispin, and Booth left saying he wanted his old life back, and I haven't seen him. Not that I would out here..."

Nova rolled her eyes. Nausea churned in her stomach. She pushed on with her story while she still could.

"I did my routine skydive with my jump buddy, but his chute failed. He crashed into me. Thank God, because it kept him from...well, we finally got untangled, and he got his reserve out but...I don't know if he made it because the wind dragged me through the fire and right over a cliff." She paused.

Her breaths came in shallow pants that burned her broken ribs.

Henry cocked his head. "I'm assuming this is where the mountain lion comes in?"

She didn't have it in her to do anything but nod.

"Now, that's quite a tale." Henry scratched his chin. "So this smokejumper Homeland agent...Booth, you said. He's taking care of Crispin?"

"I...I guess." Her head swam with dizziness. Whatever adrenaline had kept her going was waning. She couldn't—

Nova's legs folded under her.

Henry caught her. "Okay, girlie. We best get you someplace where you can get some water and rest."

She didn't protest when Henry scooped her up, but her body did. Her breath caught, which sent lightning bolts of pain screaming through every muscle. She heard Henry grunt and then nothing at all.

ELEVEN

THE TRIP BACK TO EMBER PASSED IN A HAZY BLUR. Booth clenched the steering wheel and pressed the gas pedal flat to the floor. He darted his eyes between the road and the rearview, expecting to spot Floyd or one of his men.

On the seat beside him, Crispin either slept or faded in and out of consciousness, his breaths shallow and uneven. His skin was pale, and beads of sweat dotted his forehead. Probably had an infection in his surgical wound.

There was so much to talk about, but Booth let his friend rest. There'd be time once he'd been treated.

Crispin moaned, eyes rolling underneath paper-thin eyelids. Booth pressed the gas harder.

Ember Memorial Hospital emerged up ahead.

He skidded the truck to a stop under the emergency awning, ignoring the No Parking signs. Engine running, he flung open the truck door and hopped out. He raced around the front of the truck and through the ambulance bay doors.

"Hey! You can't park there!" a nurse called.

"It's an emergency. I need a wheelchair. I have a patient in bad shape."

"We've got this," the nurse said.

Orderlies grabbed a gurney and followed Booth back to the truck. He stood there watching as they loaded Crispin's limp body and shouted orders to each other.

Booth followed them inside. He wanted to help. Do something besides watch the doctors and nurses.

A nurse approached, eyes soft with empathy. "You did the right thing bringing him here. We'll do everything we can for your friend."

Booth nodded. He stared at Crispin's motionless form. Why hadn't he stayed at the hospital with him in the first place? Crispin had needed him, and he'd left his partner behind to go fight a fire.

But then, if he hadn't been there, how many of his fellow smokejumpers would've died? Nova included.

The gurney turned into a room. "Wait right there." The nurse gestured to a nearby chair and pulled the curtain, blocking his view.

The medical staff exchanged orders and vitals over the beeping and humming of medical equipment.

Booth was too amped to sit. He paced the tiled floor, torn between staying by Crispin's side and the gnawing need to go find Floyd. And what about Nova? She needed him. The town needed him. What was he supposed to do? He couldn't be in three places at once.

He raked a hand through his hair.

This yo-yoing between his old life and his new one had to stop. Everything within him wanted a life with Nova, but how could he with The Brothers still out there?

He'd have to choose.

Nova or Crispin.

Sheriff Hutchinson strode toward Booth, hand resting on his holstered sidearm. A deputy trailed a step behind.

The sheriff stopped and cocked a sideways grin. "Trouble seems to follow you around, don't it, son?"

Booth shot him a glance. "More like I'm chasing trouble."

The sheriff crossed his arms over his barrel chest. "Care to fill me in?"

He recounted everything, starting with Crispin leaving the hospital. Hutchinson listened, pausing Booth to ask for clarification now and again.

When he'd finished, Hutchinson unfolded his arms and adjusted his hat. "Floyd wants something from you, Booth. This isn't just about revenge."

Booth clenched his jaw. The sheriff needed more information if Booth expected him to help at all. More—not all. "Floyd's after information. Something he thinks Crispin and I know about Henry Snow."

"Henry Snow? That's a name from the past. What does Floyd want with him?"

"He believes Henry has something. A missile, some weapon. And he's willing to go to extreme lengths to find it."

The sheriff's eyes narrowed. "And he thinks you know where Snow is?"

Booth nodded. "He doesn't care what he has to do to find out. Including setting that fire in the jump base and nearly killing Crispin."

Had Crazy Henry really hidden a nuke, one The Brothers desperately wanted to find so they could start a war?

No wonder Nova hadn't believed his stories were true.

"Do you? Know where Snow is, I mean." Hutchinson arched a brow and turned his ear a little toward Booth.

"I don't know how to contact him or where he is right now." Booth glanced at the deputy scribbling in his notebook. Booth wasn't quite ready to tell Hutchinson that Henry was definitely somewhere in the Kootenai National Forest. But could he find the old coot?

Doubtful.

If Henry didn't want to be found, no one would ever see him.

The sheriff straightened. "I'll post a deputy at Crispin's door, keep an eye on your friend. No one in or out except medical staff. We'll also send someone out to investigate that cabin."

If it was still there. At least his fire line would prevent the fire from spreading into the forest.

"Appreciate it, Sheriff." Booth read the address from his phone. "It might give you a lead on Floyd."

Hutchinson's gaze lingered on Booth. "If Floyd is trying to use Crispin as leverage against you, it's best you keep your distance. Let us handle this."

Booth clenched his hand into a fist. After all Floyd had put him through—put Crispin and Nova through...He shook his head. "I can't just sit back—"

The man clapped a firm hand on his shoulder. "Sometimes, Booth, the best way to protect those you care about is to let the law do its job. We'll find Floyd and put an end to this."

With those words hanging in the air, Booth

watched as the sheriff and his deputy walked away. There it was again.

His old life was law enforcement. He wouldn't stay idle. He'd find Henry Snow before Floyd did and take down The Brothers for good.

First, though, he had to find Nova…

Booth's boots squeaked on the hospital's polished floors as he hurried toward the exit.

He halted at the sight of JoJo Butcher huddled in the ER waiting room. Tears streaked her face. His pulse quickened. If JoJo was here, that meant something had gone terribly wrong out there.

"JoJo?" Booth lowered himself onto the chair beside her. "Why aren't you with the others?"

She turned puffy red eyes on him. "There was an accident on the jump. Finn and Nova…they collided midair." She choked on a quiet sob. "Finn's hurt pretty bad and…and they can't find Nova."

His breath fled his lungs.

JoJo dragged a sleeve across her wet cheeks and nodded. "Some spotter crews are still out there, but visibility is terrible, and the fire's spreading so fast…" She lifted her shoulders in a helpless shrug. "They said the odds aren't very good."

"I want you to pray. It's the best thing we can do. I'm learning that true redemption lies in surrendering every situation to Jesus. Even this one." Booth gave her shoulder a squeeze and stood. Already calculating the fastest route to jump base, he figured he could be airborne with the next smokejumper team in twenty minutes. "I'm going to find Nova."

"You can't. Last chopper just left to evacuate the jumpers. Ground crews have pulled back too." She lifted red-rimmed eyes. "Aria's waiting at jump base in case…"

In case they found more jumpers to recover than survivors.

He should've never left Nova.

"I'm not giving up on her." He headed for the door. "The storm has grounded planes, not me. I'll get there on foot if I have to."

Nova turned her head and sucked air between her teeth. Pain thrummed in her skull and every other part of her. She opened her gritty eyes, blinking against the blurriness.

That had been some dream. Falling into a hole like Alice and coming face-to-face with—

"Oh, hey. You're awake," said Henry's voice.

Crazy Henry.

It wasn't a dream.

"Easy there." Henry sat in a ratty old recliner, watching her from across the room. "You blacked out back there, but you're safe now."

Nova attempted to sit up. Her body protested every movement. "Where am I?"

"My hideaway." Henry leaned forward. The metal springs on his chair squeaked. "Needed a quiet place to tend to your injuries and let you get some rest."

She glanced around the windowless room, a modest space with a worn sofa and a simple kitchen setup. A fire burned in a stone hearth. The chimney had been carved up from the cave wall.

"Thank you for carrying me out of there." Now she just needed to get to a hospital.

Henry handed her a steaming cup of tea that smelled amazing. "Let's call it even. Do you remember what you said before you blacked out?"

Heat crept up her neck. Oh, she remembered all right. That little word-vomit episode in the tunnel right before she'd passed out. "I remember."

Henry's sharp and weathered eyes flickered with concern. "If what you're saying is true, we're all in more danger than you can imagine."

Nova shifted on the sofa. "Tell me."

"Earl and Floyd Blackwell are biological brothers, but they're also a new division of an organization, called The Brothers in northwest Montana. Russian sympathizers, but they want to start a war that will destroy America so Russia can be the world power. Their dad was a Russian spy in the US and was killed by me a few years ago."

A shiver ran down her spine. Booth had told stories of Crazy Henry killing a Russian spy. "Why are they after Crispin and Booth?"

"If they prove themselves, they'll get an invite to make the Bratva. They've made themselves legitimate players in their world. They believe finding a missing nuke—rumors their dad must've told them—will be their ticket. They're willing to do anything to prove themselves to the Russians."

Nova's mind whirred. This was way more than stories. It was a real-life geopolitical game with lives at stake.

"Earl's dead," she said. "He died in a wildfire. Floyd probably wants to avenge his brother's death."

Henry's features hardened. "Floyd won't stop until he gets what he wants. He'll be even more dangerous. And right now, he's got a hired group of assassins at his disposal."

"Assassins?" Nova's heart pounded at the mention of more men coming after Crispin and Booth. "Are you kidding?"

"I wish I was. I've been listening to some radio chatter, intercepting phone conversations. Things are only escalating."

"We need to warn them, Henry." She wrapped an arm around her aching ribs. How far could she get in this condition?

Henry's expression mirrored her concern. "There is no *we*, Nova. We're dealing with a different kind of danger here. The moment I step outside, Russian satellites will be snapping pictures faster than the paparazzi. That's why no one has seen me in years—other than you firefighters the past few weeks." He shook his head. "Always landing in trouble."

Her mind raced for a solution. "We can help you. Booth needs to know you're here. We can't let Floyd's hired guns catch him off guard."

"Just hold on." He held up a palm. "We need to tread carefully. If what you said is true and Floyd's closing in on the nuke, Booth might be the key to saving Crispin and stopping Floyd."

The room seemed smaller. The air thickened, making it hard to breathe. Her eyes bored into Henry's. "Th-th-the nuke? It's…here?"

Henry's gaze held hers for a beat.

She looked around the room. What was she expecting? To see it leaning against a wall? "Okay, forget that. What's Booth got to do with it? He only found out Crispin was alive a few days ago."

"I'm the one who sent Booth to live here. He's

been doing some searching of his own, and he knows how to stop The Brothers. I need you to be the one who warns him."

"Sure, but I lost my radio and phone—"

Henry shook his head. "This can't go over any wires. No phones. No email. Tell him in person. Quietly."

"But how? We're trapped by the wildfire. Even if we weren't engulfed by flames, I'm in no condition to hike back up the mountain."

A small smile tugged at Henry's lips. "Don't you worry about that. I've got a few tricks up my sleeve. There's a way to navigate around this chaos."

Her brow furrowed. He'd said the firefighters had seen him. "Wait...the old mining house! I knew I saw someone in there. That was you?" Nova's eyes widened. The metal ring on the floor. "You had a trapdoor. That's how you escaped the fire."

"One of many I have scattered all over the place. There's a way to navigate this wildfire without succumbing to it."

"You have a way to get me home safe?"

"It won't be easy, but it's our best chance." Henry stood and moved toward the door. "Sit tight. I'll be back."

Henry disappeared into the darkness, leaving Nova alone with the crackling flames in the fireplace.

As Nova awaited Henry's return, she assessed her injuries. A white bandage covered the cut on her forearm. Henry had wrapped her ankle with an elastic bandage and built a makeshift splint to support her possibly broken ankle.

The tea had dulled the pain pulsing through her

body. A second cup might help, but she doubted she could even stand.

She took a steadying breath and leaned back on the pillow. Her thoughts coalesced into a prayer.

"God, I need Your peace. I...I can't do this on my own. I need You," she whispered. "Help me find Booth. Warn him about all this. Keep him safe."

The door creaked open, startling Nova awake.

Henry's presence filled the room. "Ready to find your way home again?"

"More than ready." She had to find Booth and check in with her crew. Had to know if Finn had survived...or not.

"Okay, up we go." With Henry's support, she managed to get off the couch. She took a beat to gather her bearings. "Keep weight off your foot as much as you can. We've got a bit of a walk. Use these." He handed Nova a pair of ancient-looking crutches.

Henry grabbed a flashlight and led Nova down a darkened tunnel. It was slow going with her injuries, but not as bad as she'd expected.

He turned left at a T intersection, walked awhile, and turned right at the next. Then another right and a left. Henry had her all turned around, and she was pretty sure they were walking right back to where they'd started.

Up ahead, an ominous glow illuminated the mouth of a cave. The silhouette standing at the opening froze her in place.

Henry stopped beside her. "What? What's wrong?"

"Is that...?"

He shone the flashlight at the opening.

A saddled horse stood tethered and waiting. It lifted its head and whinnied.

Oh…oh no. Henry expected her to ride that horse.

Ride through the wildfire to safety.

Her good leg began to tremble, and her possibly broken ankle throbbed. "No way, Henry. I can't ride that horse."

"You don't know how to ride?"

"It's not…I can't do it." She leaned against the cold stone of the cave wall.

Henry put a warm hand on her shoulder. "Listen, kid. I'm not sayin' it's going to be easy. Especially in your condition. But it's the only way. No vehicle can do what Abilene can do."

"Abilene?" Nova looked at the horse. Henry was right. It was her only way out of the wildfire.

Her only way to find Booth before Floyd did.

She crutched over to Abilene. Reached up and petted her muzzle.

This wasn't the same as what'd happened before. She wasn't a frightened child leaving her family behind. This was her opportunity to do what Booth had done for her—save his life.

The fire's roar outside the cave intensified. Abilene didn't flinch. Didn't shuffle her feet. She stood strong.

Nova squared her shoulders.

She met Henry's gaze. "I'll do it. I'll ride out."

Henry gave a sharp nod. "You can do this, Nova. Trust the horse. Trust yourself. Trust God."

As he helped her onto the saddle, Nova felt the familiar rhythm of the horse beneath her. Trust in the plan. Stay safe. She could do this.

"How do I know where to go? I don't even know where I am."

Henry untied the reins and handed them to Nova. "Don't worry, Abilene knows the way. You've got some supplies in her saddlebags." Henry stepped back. "Now, go on. Get."

She smiled at Henry. "Thank you."

Nova split the reins and turned Abilene around to face the flaming wilderness outside.

Fire licked at the edges of her vision. A wall of heat and smoke crowded in. It wasn't too late to turn back around.

No.

Nova nudged Abilene forward. The horse moved with a grace Nova hadn't expected. The fire loomed ahead. Nova's heart echoed the rhythm of the horse's hooves.

Things were different. This time, she wasn't leaving a loved one behind.

She was riding toward him.

Did she…? Yes. She did love Booth.

Against all odds, she would find a way to him—the man she loved. Together, they'd face whatever challenges awaited them beyond the flames.

TWELVE

FLOYD'S TRUCK SCREECHED TO A STOP NEAR THE airplane hangar at jump base, and Booth jumped out. He slammed the truck door with a clang. Scanning the area, he spotted Aria and jogged toward her.

"I need that next plane out." His breathing was labored. "Have to get back to the fire."

Aria's eyes clouded and she glanced down. "Booth, it's bad out there. You heard about what happened to Nova?"

He gave a terse nod. "JoJo told me. That's why I need to go up with the crew. I have to find her."

Aria shook her head, her ponytail swaying with the motion. "Booth, there is no crew! The wind is too unpredictable right now. It's too dangerous for jumping. Retardant planes are doing their runs, and the search-and-rescue choppers are scouring the area. Miles hasn't given the green light for a new crew yet, and I'm grounded until he decides it's safe enough for anyone to jump."

Booth scrubbed a palm across his tired face. Nova might be out there, injured or worse, and she mattered more than protocols. "I can't just sit here, Aria. I have to find her."

Studying him, she said, "You're in love with Nova, aren't you?"

"Yeah, I am. More than I ever thought possible." He swallowed. Blinked against visions of Nova's broken body obscured by smoke and flame.

No. She was a survivor. He had to believe that.

A seismic shift moved deep within.

Booth let go of some of the tension that had haunted him. All this time, he'd been torn between his past as a Homeland Security agent and the new life he'd found with the smokejumpers. Nova was the bridge between the two. He could see that now.

No matter where he stood—no matter who he was—he loved her.

"Please, Aria. Let's go look for her." He tucked a hand in his pocket and dipped his head. "I love her. I can't lose her."

Aria nodded. "Nova's my best friend. It was killin' me to sit here. You're just the push I needed. We'll scour every acre if we must."

Booth shifted the focus back to the immediate crisis. "Can you fly in these winds?"

Aria adjusted her baseball hat by lifting it and putting it back on her head. "I can, but Booth, it's risky. The winds are unpredictable, and it's not like I'm flyin' an F-35."

"I won't jump unless it's safe. I need to find her. Please, Aria."

She chewed the side of her lip. "All right. I'm probably going to get fired for this, but I could use a change of scenery anyway."

"Thank you!" He hugged her. "I don't want you to lose your job, but really. Thank you."

"Okay, okay." She patted his shoulder. "Let's get moving."

"I'll grab my gear while you do your checks."

Aria cast a hard look at him.

"Just in case," he said. "Always gotta be prepared."

Booth ran to the ready room and found a spare set of Nomex pants and shirt and changed into them. He pulled on his padded jumpsuit and his parachute gear. On his way out, he grabbed a helmet, skipping all the extras he normally stuffed in his pockets.

He'd only jump if he found Nova and conditions were right.

Back at the plane, Aria had torn through preflight checks in record time and was ready for takeoff. "Strap in."

He climbed inside and buckled in next to her.

The propellers of the DHC-6 Twin Otter roared to life.

As Aria piloted them up into the swirling darkness, Booth prayed. "God, Nova's probably out there alone and injured. I need to find her. Help her get home. Please keep her safe from the fire and any other danger she might face."

Like Floyd.

In the cockpit, Aria focused on navigating violent currents causing intense turbulence. Gale-force winds buffeted the wings as she fought to hold course for Nova's last coordinates.

As Booth peered through the haze, his stomach twisted from more than airsickness. A sea of orange and black stretched as far as he could see. Flaming tongues consumed everything in their path.

Somewhere down in that fiery wasteland was the woman who held his heart.

The plane descended toward the last known location of Nova's jump. It was difficult to see in the darkness, but the flames still burned hot beneath them.

"She's a survivor," Aria yelled over the plane's engine. "We just have to find her."

If she could still be found. Wildfires didn't care if she was the strongest woman he'd ever known. That she'd endured the nightmare of riding away from a fire, leaving her parents to perish. That she'd emerged with a heart burning to help save lives from the very thing that had stolen her family.

No, he couldn't lose hope. Not when he'd just found true purpose again. God had redeemed him. Given him a new life—the life he really wanted despite all the running and hiding. "She's down there somewhere. I know it."

Gripping the radio, Aria switched to command's operational channel. "Jump Two checking in. Currently en route to recent search sector three on a recovery mission."

Miles's gravelly voice crackled through. "Aria, what're you doing out there? Winds are still erratic. You do not have permission for this."

Aria kept them on course through an updraft's jolt. "Extra pair of eyes on the ground. We're not jumping."

"You darn well better not be." He paused. "Go ahead. We won't have clearance for jumpers for a few hours yet. Logan's coordinating the search and rescue on the ground."

"Copy. Switching to the SAR frequency for now." Aria toggled over and nodded to him. "Go ahead and check in. I need to focus."

Booth held the call button. "Logan, it's Booth. What's your team's status?"

Static hissed before Logan's smoke-raw voice came on. "We've got three crews working a grid pattern where Nova went down. No flare sightings or radio contact so far." He hesitated. "It was an inferno tearing through. Odds aren't favorable that—"

"Don't. Don't say it." Booth choked on the words.

He cleared his throat. "Did teams confirm if she got her shelter deployed?"

"Negative. JoJo saw her chute catch fire before losing sight completely."

Booth scrubbed a palm down his face, beating himself up all over again. Why hadn't he stopped Nova from going on that jump? Or gone with her? At least they'd have been together right now.

Hindsight shredded his heart.

Sheriff Hutchinson's words echoed in his mind. *Sometimes, Booth, the best way to protect those you care about is to let the law do its job.* He was right.

He ran a hand through his disheveled hair. "I should've stayed with her. She needed me, and I walked away."

Aria shot him a glance. "We'll find her. Just stay focused."

Booth turned and looked out the window. Images of Earl's charred remains popped unwanted into his head.

Sure, he might find Nova, but what if he was too late?

Nova urged Abilene forward. Her hands gripped the reins as the horse navigated the uneven terrain in darkness. She let Abilene lead the way. The horse picked her way through the underbrush, maneuvering around rocks and fallen branches.

Henry had said to trust the horse, and that's what she was doing. She had no other choice because she was tired, hungry, and utterly lost.

"I trust you, Abilene." Nova patted the horse on the neck. "And I trust You, God."

A branch whipped past Nova's temple. She winced and pressed her bandaged arm to the sting. A thin line of blood bloomed on the bandage. "Okay. That wasn't your fault, but I'd appreciate it if you didn't drive me into the branches."

Abilene nickered in response.

The forest around them was alive with the crackle of approaching wildfire. The scent of burning wood and the distant roar of flames hung in the air like a warning.

Another rib-jostling stride caused Nova to clamp her jaw tight, stifling a groan. Pain blazed from her ankle, but she dared not slow Abilene.

The makeshift splint provided some support, but she couldn't put any weight in the stirrup. Abilene's every step sent sharp pangs radiating up her leg and through her ribs.

The horse seemed to sense her condition and

moved with a deliberate slowness that allowed Nova to endure the ride.

As they moved, Nova's mind raced with thoughts of Booth.

The information Henry had shared sounded like another ultrafantastical story. The Brothers. Russian sympathizers. Revenge. A missing nuke...It was hard to comprehend the magnitude of the danger they faced.

She couldn't shake the image of Booth standing in the crosshairs of assassins, oblivious.

An ominous glow lit up the sky where the wildfire raged, creeping closer by the hour. Nova had no doubt the flames would soon find their way to her. She'd been considering how to outrun the fire's advance, same as every wildfire.

Her shoulders knotted, imagining fire nipping at Abilene's heels. She reached out and stroked the horse's neck. "Don't worry, girl. We'll find our way."

As if in response, Abilene jerked her head and swished her tail.

Then another sound broke the quiet rhythm of the horse's hooves. Was that...

A plane engine rumbled in the distance.

Her gaze snapped upward, scouring the bare snatches of sky visible through breaks in the canopy.

The plane droned overhead. Nova's heart raced. She needed to be seen, to attract attention and bring help. Signaling the plane meant rescuers could fly Nova back to the base.

Back to Booth.

Her grip tightened on the reins. She dug one heel into the horse's side, urging the mare into a jolting canter. "C'mon, girl. Giddy up."

Abilene responded. Hooves thundered through the underbrush.

Nova's pain intensified as Abilene picked up the pace.

Low-hanging branches whipped past Nova's face, and she hunched low over the horse's neck, using her uninjured leg to grip the barrel of Abilene's body.

They broke through a copse of trees into a wide meadow. Nova hauled back on the reins, chest heaving from the effort of staying astride.

She scanned the sky for the passing plane.

Overhead, the plane's beacon lights flashed in the inky black sky.

Heart thrashing, she let out a howl. "Nooooo!" The plane was flying away from her.

She'd missed it.

Her mind raced with possibilities. Maybe it wasn't too late to signal them. But how?

Fumbling with the saddlebags, Nova located two emergency flares. Striking them alight, she tossed the sputtering red fuses into the field, where they glowed red. This had to work. Had to catch the pilot's eye.

Abilene shifted beneath her.

"It's okay. They'll come back." They'd have to.

Gritting her teeth, Nova awkwardly dismounted. She half slid, half fell from the saddle and landed hard on the ground with a strangled cry. Her body gave out and she collapsed. The impact jarred her broken ribs. She curled on her side, panting.

Flare smoke wafted overhead.

Nova forced herself to rise, clinging to the stirrup for balance. On legs that threatened to buckle, she hobbled to the saddlebags and searched the pouches for more flares but only found a flashlight.

Yes. This could work.

Nova flipped on the flashlight beam. Limped into the open field. Sank to her bottom in the meadow between the two flares.

In the hazy red light of the beacons, she waved the flashlight overhead in broad arcs.

"Hey! I'm down here!"

They couldn't hear her, of course, but she shouted and signaled for help anyway. "Come back! Come back!"

A tear slipped free as she watched the plane disappear through the haze. "Please...please see me... I need help."

THIRTEEN

Aria banked them toward the foothills devastated by flame.

Through the smoke's haze, Booth glimpsed a search crew working downhill. Tiny insects combing a moonscape of char for any sign of their fellow smokejumper.

Jaw rock hard, Booth scoured the terrain as Aria circled wide.

They'd been searching for thirty minutes when the radio crackled.

"Aria, I need you back at the base." Miles's voice broke through the static. "The next round of smokejumpers can deploy within the hour." He filled her in on the new plan to stay ahead of the fire and keep it from reaching Snowhaven if possible.

"Copy, we'll turn back," Aria said.

"And Aria?" Miles lowered his voice. "Tell Booth I'm sorry, but we've called off the search for now. We need all hands on deck."

The news hit Booth like a gut punch. He turned to Aria, not sure what to say. Not sure the words would form if he tried.

She glanced at him. "I'm sorry, Booth. We have to give up the search for now..." Her voice trailed off. She sounded distraught.

Booth could relate.

He nodded. "I get it. It's not your fault. You're following orders."

The embers of hope that had burned within him began to fade. A cold emptiness took its place.

He understood the decision, though. Snowhaven had hundreds of lives in the path of the fire. No one liked to leave a man behind, but if they didn't pull the crews now, they'd risk losing the town.

Booth sighed. He knew what he had to do. What Nova would want him to do. "All right. Let's head back. I'll go out with the next crew and help with the fire."

Aria pressed her lips together and nodded.

The plane turned, making a wide loop around the Kootenai mountains. Booth's gaze was fixed on the darkness below. He couldn't shake the feeling that they'd been so close to finding her.

Nova was out there somewhere in the vast expanse of burning forest.

Halfway back to the jump base, Booth caught a sudden flash of light in the distance. His heart skipped a beat.

He all but jumped out of his seat. "Did you see that?" He pointed as he strained to see through the darkness.

Aria squinted. "I saw it. What was that?"

"It's Nova!"

"Are you sure? It could be—"

"No, look!" Booth unbuckled and leaned over to point to the spot. "In that clearing down there. See the red glowing dots? Those are flares. The fire's way over there."

Aria's eyes went wide. "Look!"

Booth watched as a white light flashed between the two flares. Three short flashes, then three long flashes, followed by three short flashes. "It's an SOS. It's Nova! She's signaling for help."

Her mouth fell open. "Thank You, Lord. We've found her..."

Booth stood. "Take us up to three thousand. I'm going down there."

Aria nodded. She guided the plane upward and radioed Command.

Booth headed to the back as Aria updated Miles and gave him Nova's coordinates.

A flood of adrenaline coursed through his body at the possibility of rescuing Nova. His breaths came rapid and shallow. The chest strap on his harness pressed tight.

He took a steadying breath. Now wasn't the time to get frazzled. He'd be no good to Nova if he lost focus and messed up his jump.

The plane ascended, leaving the burning forest below. Booth hooked up his drogue static line. Completed his four-point check. Took another breath and readied himself for the jump.

"No time for streamers tonight," Aria's voice announced over the intercom. "Winds are still tricky, so be ready for anything. The jump spot's in that little meadow just south of the fire, where Nova's lights are. Do you see it?"

"I see it!"

He stepped closer to the door and braced himself. Yanked the handle and let the door swing back, careful not to get sucked out by the slipstream. Smoke-filled wind roared in.

Aria glanced over her shoulder. "Get ready!"

Booth took his place in the door. One toe of his boot stuck out over the edge. He looked down at the darkness and inhaled a deep breath, then released it.

"Get ready, Wildfire Girl. I'm comin' for you."

She was spent. Nova wasn't sure how long she'd sat in the grass with tears rolling down her face, clicking the flashlight in an SOS pattern, before Abilene shuffled over.

The horse nudged her ear and mouthed her tangled hair.

Nova dropped the flashlight in her lap and scratched Abilene's chin. "Thank you. I think I was starting to spiral a little. I guess they're not coming back, so we'd better figure out what to do."

Abilene still knew the way home. Or so Henry had assured her.

Okay, but how would she haul herself onto Abilene's back with a broken ankle? Did she even have enough left in her to ride out, or would pain and exhaustion force her to fall?

A familiar pressure built in Nova's chest, crushing her lungs like a vise. Her next inhale emerged shallow and ragged. Closing her eyes didn't block out the suffocating wave of pain.

No one is coming back. You will die here. Forgotten.

"No," she choked out through gritted teeth. Aria's words replayed in her head. *I love you and you have a whole crew that loves you—in their own way. No one will ever forget you, Nova Burns.*

Sagging forward onto one palm, Nova pressed the other hand hard over her galloping heart.

Mind over matter.

Nova raised her head and forced heavy eyelids open.

She was trained for worst-case wilderness scenarios. This was just another mission requiring her resolve and survival skills.

She hadn't lost it all yet.

Abilene whinnied and lifted her muzzle.

Nova heard it too. The growing thunder of an approaching engine.

She scrambled for the flashlight and thumbed it on, off, on, off…

The night sky overhead flashed with her SOS. "Please…this time, see me."

The plane cruised back into view, this time flying higher. Any smokejumper would recognize the aircraft positioning.

"I knew it," she told Abilene. "We're getting out of here!"

She tracked the plane's path. Her heart nearly jumped out of her chest when the beacon light flashed and she caught a glimpse of the open door.

When the lone figure launched into open space, Nova sucked in a breath that squeezed her ribs.

Too much depended on the next few seconds. She forgot to breathe, watching the skydiver's trajectory.

After gut-wrenching seconds, the parachute canopy deployed. Nova used Abilene for support and pulled herself up to standing.

She tracked the form's descent. Swirling wind spilled air from the canopy and the jumper plunged.

The jumper hit the ground with bruising force. Fabric billowed behind him as he rolled through the landing. From fifty yards away, she watched the man wrestle clear of the deflated rigging, stand, and toss his helmet on the ground. He whipped in her direction.

Nova released her pent-up breath in an explosive rush.

The lines of the muscular silhouette sent her pulse thrumming. She heard someone sob his name. Then realized that the broken cry had come from her own throat.

"Booth!"

Every fiber of her wanted to run to him, but her ankle screamed in protest.

Booth sprinted through the grass. "Nova! Nova!"

Disheveled and smoke-stained, he was still the most beautiful sight she'd ever seen.

And he was here. Impossibly here. Striding toward her with that wide grin on his face.

Then his arms enveloped her. Bonds of warmth and muscle that felt like coming home.

Despite her pain, Nova clutched him. Breathed in his scent. Nuzzled the soft whiskers on his jaw. This was no pain-induced hallucination. He'd really come for her.

"Thank God. I've been going crazy looking for you," Booth rasped. One broad hand brushed her tangled hair.

Nova withdrew enough to angle her face up. "I'm so glad it was you."

His searching gaze took in her features. "Are you hurt? How bad?"

"Nothing serious." Nova dismissed her aching injuries. She didn't want to waste another second not touching him. She framed his face in her palms. "I can't believe you found me. By some miracle, you're really here."

His arms tightened. "I couldn't stop—wouldn't stop—until I found you."

She smiled even as emotion clogged her throat. Nova lifted her mouth to meet his. She fisted her hands in his shirt, pulling herself closer. Booth kissed her until she thought she might melt into him.

Heart hammering, Nova eased back. Booth kept one arm around her. The other hand traced her cheek tenderly.

"I never want us separated like that again. When I heard you'd disappeared in the fire..." Deep lines creased his brow.

"I started thinking no one would ever find me. Especially not you. How could you possibly have tracked me to the middle of nowhere?"

"God. It had to be God leading us here." Booth looked up at the plane passing overhead. "Aria and I went a little rogue, but we can talk about it later. Speaking of..." Booth pulled his radio out of his pocket and confirmed he'd found Nova alive and well.

The call came back with cheers and promises that a chopper would be there to pick them up in less than thirty minutes.

Nova pressed impulsive kisses across his jaw. His chin. His lips. "I love you. Beyond life itself. I'm sorry for being so pushy—or bossy. Whatever. I can do better. I will do better."

"I love you too. Just the way you are." He pressed a kiss into her forehead. "I've got you now, and I'm not letting go."

Booth kissed her again. This time slow and gentle. She slipped her arms behind his neck and pulled him close.

When they paused for breath, Booth nodded over his shoulder. "So...what's with the horse?"

Glancing over, Nova beckoned the mare closer. She stroked her velvet muzzle while Abilene investigated Booth's shirt for treats.

"This is Abilene. My guardian, transportation, and guide."

Booth's eyebrows went up. "You? You rode this horse? I thought you hated horses."

"I don't *hate* them." She'd been terrified of what they represented in her life. Every horse had dragged up painful memories that she hadn't been able to face. "I'll admit, I didn't think I'd ever ride again after the wildfire that killed my parents. But I had to face my past if I wanted to find my way home. My father loved me so much he put me on that horse. He didn't choose me over my mom. He just chose love."

"Brave. You're so brave. How'd you figure that out?"

"I used to measure God's love by comparing what He did for me with what He'd done for another person." She paused for a shallow breath. "But that isn't right. I have to look at what God does for me, period. That's how I'll see His love. God's good all the time."

"And all the time, God's good." Booth smiled and stroked the white streak blazing down Abilene's face.

"Where'd she come from? We may need to get her home before the chopper comes."

Nova tucked herself close beneath Booth's arm and pressed her ear over his heart. The strong steady rhythm seemed to echo inside her own ribcage. "It's a long story, but I finally believe everything you've said about Crazy Henry now."

Booth looked down. "That's a bit out of left field."

"Not really. Hey, can we sit? I'm pretty sure my ankle is broken—"

"Broken? Why didn't you say so?" Flustered, Booth helped her ease down in the grass. "Let me take a look."

Nova rested her foot in his lap.

He lifted her pant leg and whistled. "That's some splint. You do that yourself?"

"No. That's where I was headed. Like I said, I believe you about Crazy Henry." She cringed as Booth pulled her pant leg back down over her ankle.

"Sorry," he said.

She dismissed it as no big deal and continued recounting everything from Finn crashing into her to being dragged off the cliff. "When I came to, the fire had blown up. I was trapped between a mountain and the forest. I stumbled around until I ran into a mountain lion cub."

Booth's eyes widened. "What?"

"The mama wasn't too happy to see me either. I was backing up when I stepped on a piece of wood covering a pit or something. Before I knew it, I was falling down an old mine shaft that caved in behind me. That's when I met Henry."

He leaned back to study her face. "You really saw Henry? Out here? You spoke with him?"

Nova nodded. "Shortly after we met, I blacked out. Somehow, I ended up in his hidey hole. A cabin built into a cave, by the looks of it. He told me he knew about you and Crispin. Told me how he'd been hiding a nuke and that The Brothers wants to find it. And if that isn't chilling enough, he said that Floyd has hired professional assassins to hunt you down and kill you."

Booth gazed into the surrounding woods. Nova sensed him processing the information. Formulating plans she couldn't begin to guess.

"I can't believe he told you everything." He ran one calloused thumb along her knuckles.

"Floyd is getting closer to finding Henry. He needed me to warn you. That's where Abilene came in."

At her name, the horse lifted her head from where she'd been grazing in the meadow.

"I walked away from that world to start a new life in a new place, but I kept looking back. Wanting to get my life back." Sighing, he tucked a strand of hair behind her ear. "I should know better by now. The past always finds a way back around eventually."

"Did you find Crispin?"

Booth nodded. "He's safe at the hospital again. Sheriff Hutchinson put a guard on the door, and he's investigating everything that happened. This man, Floyd, was behind it all. The kidnapping. The arson at jump base. The man who beat Crispin. That was all Floyd and his hired hands."

"But why?"

"Partly to get his hands on the nuke, and partly for revenge. It was his brother, Earl, that died that day at the lake when they overran us all. Floyd blames us. But he's not going to get away with it. We're going to find him and stop him once and for all."

"Good." Nova leaned her head on Booth's shoulder.

"Good? I thought you wanted me to stay out of it and let the police do their jobs."

She cringed hearing him parrot her words. "Yeah, I'm sorry about that. I didn't know—"

He kissed her. "I know."

"So, now what? Floyd isn't going to call off his assassins. He'll never stop looking for Henry."

"Can't change what's hunting me, but I can end it on my terms." His mouth flattened. "I thought I was done with my old life, but seems like it's not finished with me yet."

The thump-thump of helicopter rotors sliced through the night sky.

In a few minutes, they'd be rescued. Probably safe from the fire crowding in on them, but with the assassin still on the run, they could be walking right into the crosshairs.

FOURTEEN

TODAY WAS THE DAY. THE DAY THEY'D FIND OUT who'd be the new crew chief.

Nova shifted on the supply crate, trying to find a comfortable position for her leg encased in plaster. The crutches beside her kept slipping on the concrete floor no matter how many times she repositioned them.

The rest of the team lounged around, their usual banter muted today.

Logan and Vince sipped mugs of coffee while JoJo and Eric tapped on their phones. Booth leaned on the wall beside her.

She exhaled, blowing an errant curl off her forehead, and winced at the stab of pain in her ribs. Concern creased Booth's face, and she offered a smile despite the throbbing.

How was she supposed to lead her team when she could barely hobble across the hangar for this meeting?

At least the others had been kind, even if they couldn't stop talking about how it'd happened. They'd asked her to recount every moment in detail. She couldn't exactly tell them about Henry, but she did tell them the truth. About the midair collision, the mountain lion defending her cub, and falling down an abandoned mineshaft and breaking her ankle trying to escape a wildlife attack.

"All right, quiet down." Nova clapped her hands. "I'm back from the hospital with an update. Doctors wouldn't let me see Finn because they're worried about infection. The burns on his back and legs are severe, so they'll be keeping him in a medically induced coma a few weeks."

"Any life-threatening concerns?" Eric asked.

"It's touch and go. We'll know more in a few days, but the doc seemed optimistic," she said.

Booth squeezed her shoulder. "We'll keep praying. Won't we guys?"

Mumbles of affirmation rippled through the crew.

"How's Rico?" asked JoJo.

Nova smiled. "He's great. Charming all the nurses."

"Wouldn't expect anything else," Vince said, chuckling.

"It'll be a long recovery, but he's got a pretty good shot at coming back next season." Nova's crutch slipped again, and she grabbed for it. Missed. It clattered to the floor.

Booth picked it up. "I got you."

"Thanks." She smiled. "Can you help me out? Lean both against the wall until I need them?"

"Absolutely." Booth brushed his fingers across her hand as he collected her other crutch.

Footsteps echoed outside, followed by the

appearance of Crew Boss, Tucker Newman, sporting his own pair of crutches. Tucker's pant leg was slit to make room for the bulky cast immobilizing his knee.

"Welcome to the club," Tucker said with a wave of his crutch.

"Thanks," Nova said with a soft laugh. "If they gave frequent flyer miles for injuries, we'd have free vacations for life."

Tucker lowered himself onto a crate with a grunt. "I came to give you all an update. The wildfire has grown overnight. It's still spreading and no closer to containment. Snowhaven is in danger."

The team shared solemn glances.

"Have they evacuated the town?" asked Vince.

Tucker shook his head. "We're staying ahead of it. Struggling, but we're managing for now. But listen. The real problem is we've had some miscommunications. Too many injuries. We need some real leadership. Unfortunately, with this bum leg, I can't be out there coordinating teams—I can barely walk. We need someone calling the shots from the front lines."

He flicked a glance at Nova, then crossed his arms and looked away. "That's why Miles and I have decided on a new crew chief."

Nova stole a look at the crew. Each face seemed to be smiling at her. Coldness spread throughout her chest. This was it, wasn't it? Everything she'd worked for. Everything she'd wanted.

Tucker continued, "The new chief is someone with a lifetime of firefighting experience under her belt. She knows wildland fires and has proven herself as a real leader."

Nova sat straighter, jostling the crate. Her? Run point on a raging forest fire? Memories of orange flames and billowing smoke flashed through her mind. But also the faces of helpless residents fleeing for their lives. Her parents, trapped at their homestead. This was her chance to stop that happening again.

Her brain whirred with all the responsibilities of planning crew assignments and mapping priorities. This was the moment she'd trained for, what she'd sacrificed and bled for. A chance to channel the fire that had taken so much from her into saving others instead.

A chance to finally make her peace with the flames.

But...she didn't want it.

All she wanted was...Booth. The man who'd shown her that love conquered all. That there was more to life than hiding her heart and praying she'd never get hurt. Because when the pain came, God would always be there to give her the peace she'd so desperately sought all these years.

"Tucker, wait—" Her voice hitched.

Tucker cocked his head, eyebrows raised. The others stared.

Nova swallowed, nerves and epiphany battling as she met Tucker's gaze. "I appreciate the opportunity. It's no surprise to anyone that it's been my goal, my dream. But I think someone else should be crew chief. I...I don't want the job."

Tucker blinked. Cleared his throat. "Nova, I... um...I wasn't going to name you." He rubbed his neck, avoiding her gaze now. "I, uh, I actually already appointed someone else crew chief earlier."

"Oh." Nova couldn't restrain a nervous laugh. "Wait, you said *she* was experienced."

Everyone swiveled to look at JoJo, whose eyes were giant round question marks. "Uh-uh. Not me."

Nova looked at Tucker. "You mean there's another female candidate besides us?"

At that moment, the hangar door swung open, and a tall woman with a single dark-blonde braid down her back strode in, looking cool and collected in her incident command uniform. Her serious brown eyes scanned the room.

"Everyone," Tucker said, "meet Jade Ransom, your new crew chief."

Booth leaned against the corrugated metal of the temporary fire center, watching the sunset bathe Nova in golden light. The lingering rays danced across her red curls, setting them alight like glowing embers. All around them, cicadas trilled to life.

After the chaos of recent days, this peaceful stillness felt fragile. A momentary respite before the winds shifted again.

Nova adjusted her stance and settled the crutch pads under her arms. "So…that didn't go how I expected."

"Tell me about it." He kept his tone casual, giving her an easy out from whatever shadowed her features. "Everything okay?"

For a long moment, Nova simply studied him. Behind those deep green pools, something weighed on her. "You know, I was serious when I told Tucker I didn't want the job."

Booth blinked. "Words I never thought you'd utter. I thought this was your dream. To rise up the ranks."

"Was. It *was* my dream." The wind blew her hair across her face. She gathered it and tucked it behind her ear. "Something shifted in there. All at once I realized it's not what I want."

"So, no hard feelings about...what's her name?"

"Jade. And no. She's a fantastic smokejumper and an excellent leader. There's no one, man or woman, better suited for that role right now. I meant what I said. I'm not seeking advancement."

His eyebrows rose. All this time he'd assumed her drive to lead mirrored his own former ambitions. That familiar fire burning inside, demanding they scorch every obstacle to reach the summit of their careers.

"Well, if you're happy, then I'm happy." He couldn't help needling her a bit though. "What made the mighty Wildfire Girl change her mind about leading the charge?"

Nova's shoulders squared and she straightened on her crutches. He rubbed the back of his neck, hoping he hadn't overstepped some invisible line with her. He'd trod so carefully around the firm boundaries laid since their first meeting, and he didn't want to trigger anything that would make her erect those forbidding walls again.

"I realized there's more to life than just fighting wildland fire." Color bloomed in her cheeks. "I want to make a life...with you. That is...if your life has room for me in it."

Booth looked up, meeting Nova's steady gaze and slight smile. The sight sent his pulse hammering as her meaning crystallized.

The words, so simple yet hugely loaded, reverberated through his chest like gunfire. Heat rushed his face, and his jaw went slack.

Then Nova looked down. "Forget it, that was stupid—"

Booth crossed to her in two strides and captured her mouth with his.

She fisted one hand in his shirt. His hand cupped her cheek and traced the soft line of her jaw with his thumb. The touch sent a jolt through him.

He poured his heart into the kiss. His fear. His hope. His newfound acceptance of the past he no longer had to hide and the future he couldn't resist.

When they broke apart, Nova rested her cheek against his chest. Booth willed his heart to stop pounding so he could speak.

"Nova…" He traced her cheekbone, thumbing away a rogue tear he hoped sprang from joy, not regret. "I thought I needed to regain my old identity to find my place in this world. To be whole again."

Her eyes flickered up, pools of emerald searching his.

"I learned that my identity isn't about who I was. My true identity comes from God." He brushed back a rogue curl. "But I was so focused on what I'd been that I failed to see what I could become."

She nodded, gripped his wrist, and pressed his palm flush against her cheek.

"You were right," Booth whispered, watching her eyes drift shut again. "There is more to life than chasing flames. And I want that too. With you."

"Yeah?" A grin claimed Nova's mouth. "I dunno, you're pretty rough around the edges, Wildfire Man. Think you can keep up?"

"Count on it, Wildfire Girl." He grinned back. "Although, if you're gonna start talking sappy like that, I reserve the right to demand more kissing to shut you up."

Nova burst into laughter, scrunching her nose before hauling him back into a lingering kiss.

Far too soon, Nova drew a fortifying breath and eased back a fraction. "So...what about Crispin? How does your old partner play into this?"

Booth wished he could extinguish the hint of worry banked in her question. He feathered fingers through her tangled curls. "Crispin's still playing stubborn inmate for now. He's stayed put in the hospital with a guard protecting him while he heals up proper. Once he's mobile again...well, I guess all bets are off."

Nova didn't miss the hitch beneath his breezy tone. "But..."

Booth sighed and pressed a light kiss to her forehead. "I know Crispin. He's getting anxious to slip those leashes again," he said against her crown. "And I'm sure as Montana wildfire he'll leave me behind to go all lone wolf and chase Floyd by himself, just like every other fool notion he's had over the years."

"If he's really that determined, how do you stop someone like that? Or is this where I get ready for your disappearing act too?"

The fear laced through her wry joke hinted at the kind of pain he never wanted to inflict upon her again.

He drew back and looked down at her. "There won't be any more vanishing acts from me, Nova."

"Just like that? You're giving up your old life?"

"Not exactly." Booth sighed. "I can't promise I won't help catch bad guys. It's in my bones the way firefighting is in yours. But I can promise, no more running off and leaving you in the dark. No more secrets."

"We can have *some* secrets." Nova grinned. "Birthdays, holidays. Special surprise things like that."

"Have I told you how much I hate surprises," he murmured, pulling Nova close.

She huffed a laugh. After a long moment she asked, "What's next?"

Booth faced her fully. In her eyes he could see his future. Him on one knee with a solitaire diamond and a question. Nova in white, kissing him for the first time as his wife in front of their friends. Booth holding their first child in his arms, and Nova with sweaty red curls plastered to her face, never having looked more beautiful.

"You, Wildfire Girl. You're my future. Every sunrise and sunset from now on. You're all the future I need." One thumb brushed fiery curls from her cheek. "If you'll have me."

Nova looked up at him. Her eyes shone with understanding as her head bobbed. "Yes. A thousand times, yes."

He kissed her again, sealing their new beginning.

Booth turned them to face the sliver of sun disappearing behind the mountains.

A shiver ran down his spine.

Out there lay uncertainty. Crispin's impulsive pursuits. Floyd's unfinished agenda. Henry's hidden nuke. Even the unknown assassins still hunting the remnants of Booth's former identity.

The fight was far from over.

A fierce protectiveness surged through him, and he pulled Nova tighter. This newfound peace was too precious, too fragile.

Booth had just discovered his true identity and wasn't about to let anyone, or anything, take it away.

Thank you for reading *Fireline*! Gear up for the next Chasing Fire: Montana romantic suspense thriller, *Fireproof* by Susan May Warren. Keep reading for a sneak peek!

SECRETS. BETRAYAL. SACRIFICE.
THIS TIME, THEY'RE NOT JUST FIGHTING FIRE.

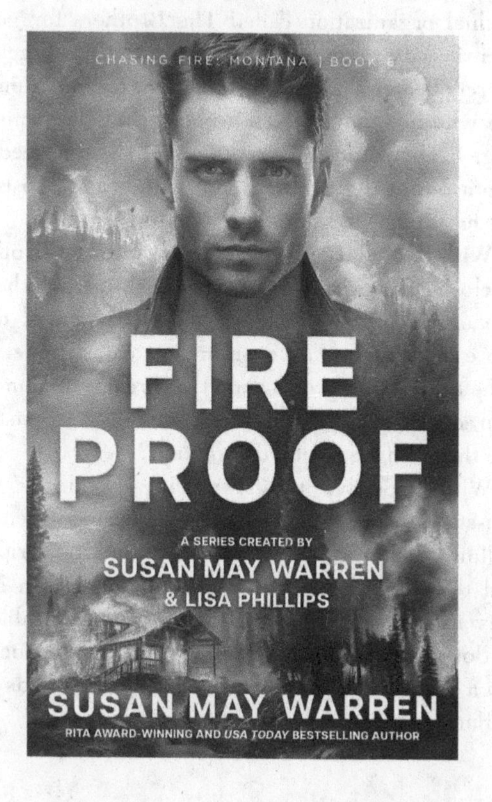

Can they save the town, find a missing nuke, and protect their hearts from getting burned?

Jade Ransom is a seasoned lead smoke jumper with something to prove. Haunted by a past mistake, she's determined to show she has what it takes to lead her own team. But on her first day fighting a raging wildfire, she rescues an injured yet mysteriously driven man from the flames—Crispin Lamb, who has even bigger problems than her.

Crispin has been secretly hunting the dangerous criminal organization called The Brothers for years. After already saving his sister from them and getting severely beaten, he's now on the hunt to find Henry, a man who may have stolen a nuclear missile from the gang. If Henry does have the nuke, Crispin needs to keep it out of the Brotherhood's hands at all costs, as they have plans to sell the weapon to Russia.

With the wildfire bearing down and The Brothers are closing in, Crispin and Jade are thrust together in a deadly race to find Henry and the potential nuke before either create an even greater catastrophe. But as their attraction grows amid the threats surrounding them, can they overcome the secrets of their pasts to save the town from total destruction?

With explosive twists, sizzling chemistry, and high-stakes danger around every burning tree, this thrilling romantic suspense will keep you gripped until the smoldering final page. Fans of Susan May Warren's epic romantic adventures won't be able to put down Jade and Crispin's race against the clock to stop a nuclear threat all while battling fiery odds and the flames igniting between them.

FIREPROOF

CHASING FIRE: MONTANA | BOOK 5

CHAPTER 1

Frankly, Crispin was just tired of being dead.

Dead, and in his pajamas.

Wow, he needed pants, because the flimsy hospital gown was getting a little breezy.

"Thanks, Kelly," he said to the night nurse as she brought in his dinner. The ever-so-delicious red Jell-O and chicken broth. Sheesh, he still had teeth, thank you, even if his insides had been a little ground up over the past week.

That's what being kidnapped and tortured did to a guy—reduced him to slurping his food.

"Eat up. I'll be back to get your blood pressure," said Kelly. Mid-thirties, no nonsense, and in a different time, different place, he'd listen to her.

But, well, he had things to do.

He pulled the tray to himself, the IV line tugging a little on the top of his hand where it connected. "Hey. Is that cop still sitting outside my door?"

"Duane? I think he went to the cafeteria for coffee. Why? You need me to call him?" She'd stopped, her hand on the door. "Do you feel unsafe? They said he was here for your protection."

Always, but, "No. I just wanted to check on the fire and the search for my attacker."

She was pretty enough. Dark hair pulled back into a low bun, wearing teal pants and a patterned shirt, the look of a mother in her expression. She wore a ring, so probably. Now she gave him a look of pity. "No. I'm sorry. Do you want me to call the sheriff and see if he's heard anything?"

"No. That's okay." He picked up his spoon. "Thanks."

He pushed away his food, leaned his head back. Closed his eyes. So close. He'd been so, so painfully, pitifully close to wrapping up this eternal, never-ending, doggone mission.

And then a biker-gangbanger slash paid assassin named Tank had to get the drop on him and rearrange his insides, looking for answers to the question Crispin still hadn't answered—*where was the nuke?*

Good question, and really, get in line, pal. Because Crispin hadn't a clue if Two-fisted Tank was an independent world-ending terrorist or if he worked with The Brothers, a.k.a. a semiorganized Russian wannabe-terrorist group conveniently working inside the American borders—also hunting for the nuke. At this point, it was a free-for-all race to find said stolen nuclear missile, and who knew how many rogue groups might be hunting down the thief, Henry Snow?

Ex-CIA agent Henry Snow, who had rescued the nuke from the grip of a rogue CIA faction and hidden it like an easter egg in the woods of Montana. The same Henry Snow who'd reached out to Crispin three-plus months ago telling him to come to Ember, Montana.

And then promptly ghosted him.

The stupid watery broth actually smelled good. Crispin reached out to pull the tray close. Heat sheered through him up his side, where at least one rib had folded under Tank's close and personal attention.

Crispin's head still hammered too, a throb that might be more like a pellet gun against his brain thanks to the go-round he'd had with kidnapper number *dos*. This time, he'd been snatched right out of the hospital, dragged to a cabin in the woods and, from his sketchy memory, might have turned to toast in a house fire if former CIA agent, and his once-upon-a-time partner, Booth Wilder hadn't rescued him.

He remembered his floppy-meat self being dragged out of danger by Booth.

But sadly, not much more until he'd woken two days ago bandaged, IVs in one arm, on oxygen, and his entire body needing a mainline of ibuprofen.

And wearing pajamas.

Agenda item numero uno: find pants.

Then he'd have to sneak past Duane and out the door of the hospital.

Lift some wheels.

Maybe connect with Booth.

And then, finally, find Henry Snow.

Not even a clue how he'd do that.

He tasted the soup. Not terrible. He finished it, slowly, letting the heat find his bruised bones. Maybe he'd live, but he'd stopped thinking past the next five minutes.

Kelly came back in. "Oh, good. I was hoping you'd eaten." She looked like she might hold up her hand for a fist bump.

He pushed the empty bowl and tray away but palmed the spoon and tucked it beside him. "Maybe next time add some real chicken?"

"Sorry. Not until the doc okays it. You had some pretty significant internal bleeding." As if to emphasize her words, she pulled down his blanket—

"Hey!" He put his hands on his flimsy gown. "I'm not sure what happened to my clothes, but—"

"Calm down, Mr. Lamb. I've seen it before. Besides, I'm just checking on your bruising."

Mr. Lamb. So, Booth had given the sheriff his sister's alias name. Felt right. He hadn't had a real name for years. Even Crispin was a nickname his sister had given him once upon a time.

He let Nurse Kelly check out his torso and caught a glimpse himself. Mostly black and purple, some green bruising. "That doesn't look too bad," he said.

She gaped at him. "You look like you've been hit by a buffalo, then trampled by the herd."

"Maybe just a couple of the calves—"

"And let's not forget you've been shot." She lifted the bandage that covered his shoulder. "Stitches are healing. Good thing it was a through and through."

Right. Good thing. He would have preferred *not* getting shot.

She examined his face. "At least your eye is open now. Better than when you came in three days ago. You're a fast healer."

Not fast enough. If he hadn't ached so much, he'd have sneaked out on day one.

"You know where my pants went?"

She reached for the blood pressure cuff. "Your clothes were handed over to the police for evidence."

Aw.

She finished, then took his pulse. "You're definitely on the mend. Although, you haven't had any visitors."

Yes, he had—a.k.a. his buddy Booth, who'd slipped in after visiting hours and given him the lowdown on Henry.

"Okay, so Floyd is still on the run. Still hunting Henry," Booth had said, his face illuminated by the moonlight cutting through the window. "And the nuke is still missing."

Crispin had been in too much pain to do anything but groan.

"But I think I have a lead on Henry. My uh...our team leader got tangled in a chute accident and went down in a cave. She said that Henry Snow rescued her."

That lit a fire inside him. "Where?"

"I have a rough map." Booth slipped a burner phone into his hand. "I'd given this to the sheriff, but after he told me today that Floyd was still out there..."

"I get it," Crispin said.

"I put the coordinates of where Nova met Henry in the phone. It's a cave north of here, in the Kootenai forest. The fire is still burning, though, so I need to go back out with the team."

"I got this," Crispin said. His voice sounded like he'd gargled with cement.

Booth raised an eyebrow. "We need help—"

"The minute we call anyone in is the minute the entire gang arrives, and suddenly we have the Lincoln

County war in Ember, Montana." He shifted and buried a groan. "I'll get out of here ASAP and find him."

Booth sighed. "You track down Henry. Then call me. Don't do this alone. I don't want to have to start a fire to save your sorry backside again." But he'd smiled. "Good to have you back, Crisp." He'd lifted a fist.

Crispin had met it. "Thanks for saving my hide."

"Twice," Booth had said. "Don't be a hero."

Right. He'd left hero behind long ago, frankly.

Now, Kelly pressed the cold face of the stethoscope to his chest. "Good news, you still have a heartbeat."

He smiled. She winked and put the scope around her neck. "Maybe another few days, and the doc will discharge you." She'd pulled out a tablet from her massive hip pocket. "I don't think the doc will let you leave without having a place to go, however."

"I have a place to go." Although, probably she meant a home, with family, so nope. Yes, his sister lived here, but he wasn't letting Tank or anyone else show up on her doorstep again, so…

"Really?" Kelly looked up from taking notes on her tablet.

"Yep. Friends in town"—sort of—"and family"—again, nope—"and I have a place north of town, well stocked." Truth. With ammo and survival supplies and everything he needed for a standoff, should the Brotherhood find him.

Again.

"My shift changes in twenty minutes, so I'll hand you off. Duane is back, but his shift is changing too." She patted Crispin's shoulder as she slipped the tablet back into her pocket. "Good thing the fire has died down in the mountains, or our bench would be leaner. Some of our nurses serve as emergency personnel on the fire line. And we're hoping for rain at the end of the week. Put an end to all this tragedy."

He nodded. "Thanks, Kelly."

She gave him a smile and picked up his tray. "See you tomorrow."

Yeah, not so much. The door closed softly behind her, and he sat up, reached for a cotton ball, and slowly pulled out his IV.

Pressed the cotton ball over the wound.

So, first thing—pants. He slipped out of bed. Then he grabbed his spoon.

Three days. Three days Floyd and his ilk had been free to hunt down Henry.

Three days. Maybe The Brothers already had the nuke.

Three days. Long enough for the Russian Bratva to set up a meet, exchange rubles for a weapon of mass destruction, and then—then it would all go down. World War Three, or at least a catastrophic terror event inside the borders of the US.

He blamed his years in the CIA for the doomsday attitude, but frankly, wasn't that what his team had given their lives to prevent? What he'd sacrificed three years of his life for?

Pants.

He poked his head out the door. Duane—big guy, clearly a Montanan with his grizzly bear girth—stood at the nurses' desk, drinking a cup of joe, chatting up the nurses: two women and a guy. Crispin remembered him—about his size, a nice guy named Nick.

Nick with pants that might fit him, stashed in the locker room down the hall.

Crispin waited until the nurses had all turned away, Duane's back still to him, and he slipped out the door, hugged the opposite wall, and stole down the hallway to the locker room door.

He'd spotted it earlier, during the obligatory get-out-of-bed-and-stroll portion of his recovery.

Now, he slipped inside. A clean room with a carpeted floor, showers, and wide lockers all with doors. *Locked* doors.

Aw.

But hanging on a hook on the wall was a pair of overalls, maybe from the maintenance crew. Bingo. He pulled them on, found a baseball hat in a cubby by the door, and added that over his bed-head hair.

No shoes, but he didn't have time to search.

He stuck his head back out into the hallway. No sign of Duane, so he just strolled out and headed toward the stairs. He took the steps down two flights to the emergency room.

Then he walked past a kid with a bloody nose, his arm pressed to his body, a woman holding a sleeping toddler, and right out under the canopy to the parking lot.

Darkness pressed against the arch of night, the last of the sunlight rimming the mountains to the north. Deep shadows draped the parking lot.

One unlocked car. He just needed one.

He walked around the lot, trying doors, ducking between cars, and—*jackpot*. Found a dinged-up orange Kia Rio and slid into the driver's seat.

Clearly the driver loved McDonald's. The car

reeked of French fries and the odor of sour milkshakes.

But Kias could be hotwired, and in moments, he'd used the spoon to take off the steering column. Then he found the ignition cylinder and shoved the end of the spoon in.

The car fired up.

Never mind that his bare foot stuck to the floor, something sticky on the gas pedal. He pulled out and headed into the night.

The firestorm was going to kill them all.

Jade stared out the open door of the Twin Otter at the fire that tipped the trees and chewed through the Kootenai forest below. Smoke billowed up, blackened and lethal, but Aria, the pilot, cleared a wide path around it just to give Jade and their spotter, a man named Duncan, a chance to test the wind, figure out how to deploy from the plane safely.

With the winds gusting in the thirty-mile-an-hour range, just getting her seven-person team—they were one firefighter short with Nova and another jumper named Rico out injured—out the door and onto the ground might be tricky.

But it didn't have to be pretty. Just safe.

Duncan sent out another check ribbon, and she watched it flutter out, then fall, then spiral, the storm of the fire grabbing it and turning it into a knot as it whisked it away.

It fell into the distant flames and vanished.

So, that didn't bode well.

"Take us higher, Aria," Duncan said and leaned away from the open door, holding on to his safety line.

Aria ascended, and Duncan closed the door. He spoke into his mic, and she heard it through her headphones. "Maybe we try to get west of it?"

It being the fire wall, headed south, toward civilization, chewing up downed lodgepole pine and the thick, dry loam of the tinder-dry forest. According to emergency response leader Miles Dafoe, the Jude County firefighters had waged war with the fire all summer since an explosion in the woods had first set off the blaze.

She'd read the fire reports on her tablet during her flight from Anchorage last night. Which meant she'd nabbed little sleep, although frankly, she'd learned to nap like a combat soldier after so many years fighting fires.

Her first real look at the blaze had come this morning as she'd walked into the makeshift Jude County fire center, located in a Quonset hut just off the runway.

Of course, she probably had "overachiever" stamped on her forehead. Or at least on the breast pocket of her jumpsuit. That's what happened when you dragged legacy everywhere you went.

But it didn't matter. They'd asked her to fill in as crew boss, and yeah, she planned to bring the house down. Keep the family name intact.

Make her big brother, Jed, proud. Maybe.

Of course, the heads of the top brass rose, and two of the three people smiled, something of warmth in their eyes.

"Jade." Conner Young, their supervisor, came over and held out his hand. "When did you get in?"

"Last night."

"Now I know we're in safe hands," Nova Burns, another legacy said. She grabbed Jade up in a hug.

"Conner said you needed a team lead after yours was hurt?" She stepped away. "How bad is it?"

"Hairline crack, really. I'll be fine. But it's a big fire—we need all the help we can get."

She looked over at the third man, tall, with dark hair, salty at the sides, wearing a green forest-service jumpsuit, his sleeves rolled up past his elbows. "This is our incident commander, Miles Dafoe."

He shook Jade's hand. "I know your brother only by reputation."

"That's enough of a threat," she said, and Miles smiled.

But she wasn't exactly kidding, was she?

Miles then pointed to a screen where a drone flew over the acres and acres of burning forest. A man who seemed in his late twenties worked the controls like he might be in a video game.

"The fire started last night—one of our pilots called it in this morning," Miles said. "We're currently fighting a blaze that's burned nearly all of central Kootenai, all the way over to County Road 518. It took out the campground and Wildlands Academy fire camp, and it even came close to a couple ranches, although we were able to save them."

He ran his hand over a map of the massive Kootenai mountain area, spread out on a wall. Tiny yellow pushpins indicated firefighters still out in the field.

"We have the fire corralled, but it's not over. And now, with this new fire pushing in from the east"—he ran a finger up South Fork Road—"if these two combine, we'll have a conflagration we won't be able to put down. It could reach Snowhaven." He ran his hand down to a red pushpin about ten miles north of Ember.

"I've been there a few times," Jade said. "Tourist town. Real population less than a thousand."

"Yes. And if the blaze gets past Snowhaven, it heads right to Ember."

"Looks like HQ already had a fire." She glanced over at the half-burnt HQ building, the front section demolished, the back draped with tarps and temporary shelter.

"Arsonist. Long story," said Conner. "But right now our focus is knocking down this fire before it joins forces with the main blaze."

"My, or rather, *your* team is ready to go," Nova said. She leaned a little on a crutch, her ankle wrapped. "They've been in for forty-eight hours—the hotshots are out with the blaze. But that area is inaccessible except by plane so—"

"Yep," Jade said. "So, we have Flattail Creek to the west, and generally, we just need to cut the fire off to the south."

"Yes. There's a small lake here—Rainbow Lake. And a creek that runs east-west. Get in, fortify a line along the creek, and use it to help slow down the blaze. We'll attack the head, too, with slurry and water from the lake, and if we can knock it down, then it's one less thing to worry about."

"What's the wind like?" Her gut tightened on the answer.

"Northwest."

Right. "I'll meet the team on the tarmac."

Nova left, and Jade loaded up her jump pockets

with a couple maps, a walkie, extra batteries, and then headed to the locker room to grab a gear bag—water, gloves, a fire shelter, space blanket, two days of MREs, a flare, and a knife. She'd already grabbed a helmet and a Pulaski and now climbed into her jumpsuit, a heavy canvas outer layer that would protect her from the heat and flames.

Should she land in the fire.

She blew out a breath. She hadn't done that since...well, since she'd been a *rookie*.

The team waited for her at the plane, doing buddy checks on their equipment. She met the pilot—Aria, dark hair, no-nonsense—and the rest of the team. Orion and Vince, a couple sawyers, and Logan, her team lead, and JoJo, a woman who also had a bit of legacy on her tail.

They got in, and Nova stood on the tarmac and waved, her face a little twisted. Yeah, Jade got that. Her worst nightmare might be sending her team out without her.

And that sounded arrogant, but they were her responsibility. And a Ransom didn't let their team down.

Thank you, big bro, for that rep.

But Jade was all in, even now, an hour later, as she stared out at the fire consuming Flatiron Mountain. It had burned around the base, approximately three miles from Rainbow Lake, and was heading southwest fast.

"Okay," she said to Duncan. "We're going to drop closer to the lake and set up along the creek. I know it's a farther hike, but there's a nice bald spot just north, and it's away from the fire." She looked at her crew, kitted up, strapped into their safety lines. "Nobody dies today."

Logan, her second-in-command, gave her a thumbs-up.

The plane banked, and Aria brought them around. Logan scooted up to Jade. "I can be first stick out with JoJo."

Not a bad idea, given the wind. If someone got blown off course, she could track them. Although, rules were, at least on her team in Alaska, crew chief went out the door first.

And she hated breaking the rules.

Still, safety first. She nodded, and as Aria descended and Duncan opened the door, Logan and JoJo lined up, first stick.

Duncan sent out a ribbon, and she watched it, her jaw tight as it fell. He looked at her and shot her a thumbs-up.

She nodded, and Logan and JoJo went out the door as she leaned over, a gloved hand on her safety line, watching.

Two chutes, deployed.

Orion and Vince jumped next. Two more chutes.

She stepped up to the door, watching.

The wind grabbed at them, but both Orion and Vince maneuvered with their toggles.

Duncan unhooked her safety line. "Be safe!"

She nodded—and jumped.

Air, brisk and full, and this—*this* was the moment that caught her up every time. The freedom, the expanse of the moment swept through her, stole her breath, told her that she might be invincible, and right now, she believed it.

Jump thousand.

Below, the flames reached for her, snapping, the wind kicking up. Logan and JoJo had already landed, a nice touchdown maybe a half mile from the blaze.

Look thousand.

She got the lay of the land—the mountain to the north, rising tall and bald, although it had nothing on the jagged beauty of the Alaska Range. A service road to the east, running northwest, cutting through the forest, a brown ribbon.

Reach thousand.

To the west, the glistening blue of the Flattail River, some twenty feet wide in areas, narrower in others. Enough, maybe, to stop the blaze.

As she drifted down, she made out a few landmarks. Wildlands Academy to the west, burnt. There went a summer full of memories.

Wait thousand.

Smoke hurtled up toward her—she'd drifted a little over the fire, the furnace tugging at her. Vince and Orion had touched earth, also in the bald spot. She glanced at the fire and pulled her rip cord.

Pull thousand.

Maybe a little soon, but the chute billowed out and caught with a jerk and a shot of pain she'd come to expect.

Then she settled into her harness and reached for the toggles.

Nothing.

She looked up. The toggles had wrapped around the risers, caught on the links. Reaching up, she caught one, tried to untangle it.

Focus. Breathe.

But the storm grabbed her, tossed her away from her trajectory.

Don't look down.

Nope. Not a chance. Below her, the fire snapped, roared, still some thousand feet below, but—

She got the toggle free. Looped it through her arm and reached for the other. No good—it was knotted around the link, not a hope of release.

The fire below her roared.

She reefed down hard on her right toggle, and the chute arched to the right, over the fire. *C'mon, c'mon.* She kept reefing, and the rig kept turning, heading east now.

She let off on the reef, and the chute straightened out, flying away from the bald spot, falling, the fire beneath her.

Still hungry.

But wind—maybe the breath of God—caught her, and she sailed over the exploding treetops, the smoke coughing up around her. Her eyes burned, but she spotted the road—

Wait. As she crossed over it, headed for the trees, she made out a car—an orange car in the ditch, the front end crushed against an electrical pole. Broken at the impact, the pole had flattened the top of the little car and fallen into the forest on the opposite side, the forest burnt and crispy.

Source of fire solved.

And then—trees. She braced herself and curled her legs up to protect them as she fell into the tangle of trees, hitting branches and crashing through leaves until she jerked, hard. Her breath shook out, her harness burned against her thighs.

She hung, swinging in the tree, some thirty feet from the forest floor.

So much for a glorious, epic first day on the job.

Looking for more more exciting romantic suspense from Sunrise Publishing?

DON'T MISS ANY CHASING FIRE: MONTANA STORIES

With heart-pounding excitement, gripping suspense, and sizzling (but clean!) romance, the CHASING FIRE: MONTANA series, brought to you by the incredible authors of Sunrise Publishing, including the dynamic duo of bestselling authors Susan May Warren and Lisa Phillips, is your epic summer binge read.

Immerse yourself in a world of short, captivating novels that are designed to be devoured in one sitting. Each book is a standalone masterpiece, (no story cliffhangers!) although you'll be craving the next one in the series!

Follow the Montana Hotshots and Smokejumpers as they chase a wildfire through northwest Montana.

The pages ignite with clean romance and high-stakes danger—these heroes (and heroines!) will capture your heart. The biggest question is...who will be your summer book boyfriend?

ELITE GUARDIANS: SAVANNAH

Safety. Secrets. Sacrifice. What will it cost these Elite Guardians to protect the innocent? Discover the answers in our Elite Guardians: Savannah series.

FIND THEM ALL AT SUNRISE PUBLISHING!

ABOUT KATE ANGELO

Kate Angelo is a bestselling Romantic Suspense author, minister, and public speaker from Southwest Missouri who works alongside her husband championing stronger marriages and families through their nonprofit. As Mom to 5 adult children, she's fluent in both sarcasm and eye rolls. Kate is a coffee addict, tech enthusiast, productivity guru, expert knitter, summer lake fanatic, prayer warrior, dog lover, avid reader, and a known klutz—just ask her doctor. Having aged out of foster care, Kate brings a unique perspective to her writing, breathing life into flawed characters who find hope and healing amidst danger. Subscribe to her newsletter to hear about her pet lion at kateangelo.com.

facebook.com/kateangeloauthor
instagram.com/kateangeloauthor
x.com/thekateangelo
bookbub.com/authors/kate-angelo
goodreads.com/kateangeloauthor
amazon.com/stores/Kate-Angelo/author/B09Q6GWHSC

ALSO BY KATE ANGELO

Vanishing Legacy

Christmas in the Crosshairs

Driving Force

Love Inspired Suspense

Hunting the Witness

CONNECT WITH SUNRISE

Thank you again for reading *Fireline.* We hope you enjoyed the story. If you did, would you be willing to do us a favor and leave a review? It doesn't have to be long—just a few words to help other readers know what they're getting. (But no spoilers! We don't want to wreck the fun!) Thank you again for reading!

We'd love to hear from you—not only about this story, but about any characters or stories you'd like to read in the future. Contact us at www.sunrisepublishing.com/contact.

We also have a monthly update that contains sneak peeks, reviews, upcoming releases, and fun stuff for our reader friends. Sign up at www.sunrisepublishing.com or scan our QR code.

MORE EPIC ROMANTIC ADVENTURE

CHASING FIRE: MONTANA

Flashpoint by Susan May Warren

Flashover by Megan Besing

Flashback by Michelle Sass Aleckson

Firestorm by Lisa Phillips

Fireline by Kate Angelo

Fireproof by Susan May Warren

MONTANA FIRE BY SUSAN MAY WARREN

Where There's Smoke (Summer of Fire)

Playing with Fire (Summer of Fire)

Burnin' For You (Summer of Fire)

Oh, The Weather Outside is Frightful (Christmas novella)

I'll be There (Montana Fire/Deep Haven crossover)

Light My Fire (Summer of the Burning Sky)

The Heat is On (Summer of the Burning Sky)

Some Like it Hot (Summer of the Burning Sky)

You Don't Have to Be a Star (spin-off)

LAST CHANCE FIRE AND RESCUE BY LISA PHILLIPS

Expired Return

Expired Hope (with Megan Besing)

Expired Promise (with Emilie Haney)

Expired Vows (with Laura Conaway)

LAST CHANCE COUNTY BY LISA PHILLIPS

Expired Refuge

Expired Secrets

Expired Cache

Expired Hero

Expired Game

Expired Plot

Expired Getaway

Expired Betrayal

Expired Flight

Expired End

www.ingramcontent.com/pod-product-compliance
Lightning Source LLC
Chambersburg PA
CBHW011307140525
26684CB00026B/213

* 9 7 8 1 9 6 3 3 7 2 1 7 5 *